the

D0779185

"I couldn't put these books down. The drama in each story—I ate it up. I felt like I lived it, like I was really there!"

— *Dymynd F.*

"Bluford books are stories that kids and teens can relate to. Readers can use them to build courage and find solutions to their problems—instead of giving up. They are a true inspiration."

— *Michelle M.*

"I want to confess something: Before I started reading the Bluford Series, I didn't like to read at all. Now I can't stop."

— *Mariela M.*

"The Bluford Series is seriously amazing. These books made me want to read more and get off my phone."

— *Ricky M.*

"I love that these books are about the hardships young people face. They show we are resilient and can overcome anything."

— *Kennedy T.*

"Each Bluford book starts out with a bang. And then, when you turn the page, it gets even better!"

— *Alex M.*

"I found it very easy to lose myself in these books. They kept my interest from beginning to end and were always realistic. The characters are vivid, and the endings left me in eager anticipation of the next book."

— *Keziah J.*

"These are life-changing stories that make you think long after you reach the last page."
— *Eddie M.*

"My school is just like Bluford High. The characters are just like people I know. These books are *real!*"
— *Jessica K.*

"For the first time in high school, I read a book I liked. For real, the Bluford Series is *tight*."
— *Jermaine B.*

"I never liked reading until I found the Bluford Series. These books have descriptions that play like high-definition movies in my head. They are fantastic and should be read by everyone."
— *Yoriell P.*

"Each Bluford book gives you a story that could happen to anyone. The details make you feel like you are inside the books. The storylines are amazing and realistic. I loved them all."
— *Elpiclio B.*

"One of my friends told me how good the Bluford Series is. She was right. Once I started reading, I couldn't stop, not even to sleep!"
— *Bibi R.*

"I love how Bluford books take risks by addressing tough topics. They may be controversial, but they are relatable to kids going through the same things. That's one of the reasons I enjoy them. They're *real*."
— *Mia M.*

The Chosen

**Karyn Langhorne Folan
and
Paul Langan**

Series Editor: Paul Langan

TOWNSEND PRESS
www.townsendpress.com

Books in the Bluford Series

Lost and Found	*Shattered*
A Matter of Trust	*Search for Safety*
Secrets in the Shadows	*No Way Out*
Someone to Love Me	*Schooled*
The Bully	*Breaking Point*
The Gun	*The Test*
Until We Meet Again	*Pretty Ugly*
Blood Is Thicker	*Promises to Keep*
Brothers in Arms	*Survivor*
Summer of Secrets	*Girls Like Me*
The Fallen	***The Chosen***

This book comes after *Survivor*.

Copyright © 2021 by Townsend Press, Inc.
Printed in the United States of America

9 8 7 6 5 4 3 2 1

Cover illustration © 2021 by Gerald Purnell

Townsend Press, Inc.
439 Kelley Drive
West Berlin, NJ 08091
permissions@townsendpress.com

ISBN: 978-1-59194-576-5

Library of Congress Control Number:
2019920646

Chapter 1

"Are you serious?" Darcy Wills's voice rose against the roar of the crowded Bluford High School cafeteria. "I thought we were gonna see each other this afternoon!"

"I-I'm sorry, Darcy," Hakeem Randall stammered. A crease appeared over his brown eyes, and his broad shoulders slumped. "I just got the job at Showtime Theater. I can't skip the f-f-first orientation meeting. Plus I got t-training—"

"Training?" Darcy grumbled. She knew his stutter meant he was stressed and that she was only adding to it, but she couldn't stop. "How hard is it to take movie tickets?"

Hakeem winced as if he'd been slapped. "C'mon, Darce. Don't be like that," he groaned. "Remember your first day at Scoops? You know how crazy it gets. They're putting me on concessions. I'll be

1

making popcorn with that nasty fake butter sauce Cooper likes. I'm s-starting on a Friday night. I need to know what I'm doing, or it'll be a disaster."

"Whatever," Darcy sighed, annoyed at how mean she sounded. "Look, I get it, but school started almost a month ago, and we've hardly seen each other. I thought things would be different this year, especially after everything that happened, you know?"

Darcy picked at the frayed corner of her notebook where she had scribbled her and Hakeem's initials during history class. She knew she wasn't being fair and that she sounded like Jamee, her sometimes whiny and demanding younger sister. But she couldn't help it. After a summer of doubts, separation, and worse, she hoped to have a fresh start with Hakeem in her junior year at Bluford High. But so far, September had only brought more interruptions and obstacles. Hakeem's new job was just the latest one.

"Maybe I should get a job at the movie theater, too. At least we could finally hang out," Darcy half joked.

"Seriously," Hakeem huffed. "Or maybe I can work at Scoops. I mean, popcorn is fine and all, but if I had to choose between the two, I'm taking ice cream any day of the week."

"Don't sound so desperate, you two," Tarah Carson chimed from across the table. "You're seeing each other next weekend, remember?" she lowered her voice and glanced toward the long cafeteria line where Cooper Hodden, her boyfriend, was waiting to get a second helping of greasy French fries. "At the party?"

The party.

Darcy nearly rolled her eyes. Tarah was throwing Cooper a surprise party for his eighteenth birthday. It was all she talked about anymore. Whenever Cooper was out of earshot, she would start rambling on about preparations. As much as Darcy liked Cooper, she was sick of hearing about his party. Last year, she and Tarah talked about everything, no matter how serious or silly, but something changed over the summer. Now Tarah only came in two flavors. She was either distant and moody or she was obsessed with Cooper's party.

She's distracted, Darcy told herself. *She'll get back to normal once the party's over.* But that day couldn't come soon enough.

"It's gonna be live, y'all! I got all kinds of food coming—all Coop's favorites. Music,

3

and a special cake. The football team's gonna be there, too. It's gonna be bigger than Homecoming!" Tarah announced for what felt like the thousandth time. "And best of all, he don't suspect a thing . . ."

Darcy watched as Hakeem rubbed his neck as if he had just strained a muscle. He shifted forward and cleared his throat nervously.

"Hold up, Tarah. About the p-party . . ." he glanced back at the cafeteria line. Cooper had just disappeared inside the serving area. "I-I'm going to have to miss most of it—"

"*What?!*"

Tarah's voice boomed through the bustling cafeteria. Heads snapped toward them for a second and quickly turned away, as if the crowd was used to Tarah's outbursts.

"Whatchu mean, you're gonna *miss* it?" Tarah leaned across the table and glared at Hakeem.

"It's my new job," Hakeem said softly. "My shifts are Friday and Saturday nights—"

"But you're his best friend!" Tarah's eyes blazed in her wide face. "You're more like a brother, especially since you're living with him now."

Hakeem had been living in Cooper's basement since the school year began.

"I know, Tarah! That's why I'm working!" Hakeem glanced over his shoulder again. Cooper still hadn't appeared. Hakeem lowered his voice, his stutter suddenly melting away the way it did when he sang. "It's not easy for Coop's mom, having another mouth to feed. I gotta pay them back somehow. Contribute, you know? He'd do the same for me."

The anger drained from Tarah's face. "But you can't miss his party, Hak. Ain't nobody else who can cover your schedule that day?"

Hakeem shook his head. "I just got the job. I can't call out already. The only reason they even hired me is 'cause I said I'd work weekends. I have to do this, Tarah. I'm sorry."

"I get what you're sayin', but no one expects you to pay," Tarah muttered. "Coop and his mom are glad to help out. They don't want your money. Especially with your dad being sick and all."

Doctors found a tumor on Hakeem's father's kidney last April. Unable to work and facing huge medical bills, he moved with the family to his brother's house in Detroit. While his health had improved a bit over the summer, he remained there with the family. Hakeem would be there too if Cooper's mom hadn't convinced Hakeem's parents to let him stay at her place so he could finish high school at Bluford. Since arriving in August, Hakeem lived in a small wood-paneled room in Cooper's basement. They called it Coop's Crib or Casa de Coop. Hakeem never complained, even though he had to share a small bathroom and duck his head every time he went up and down the steps. Darcy knew he missed his family and felt guilty for leaving while his dad was sick. But until this moment, Darcy never heard him explain why his new job was so important.

"I know they don't expect me to pay, Tarah," Hakeem answered. "But it doesn't feel right knowing how hard Cooper and his mom work. I need to do something to help them. And I'm doing it for my family too. They can't afford to be sending me money for every little thing. That's why I gotta be at work. You understand?"

Darcy felt a wave of guilt for pressuring Hakeem earlier. She wanted to apologize but held back as Tarah chewed her bottom lip, shrugged, and sighed.

"Yeah, it's just—" Tarah paused, shaking her head. "I wanted this to be perfect.

All of us finally back together. Time is flying by. We're juniors. Can you believe that?" She stared across the busy cafeteria as if she saw something that worried her. "Before long, all this is gonna be gone," she added, sweeping her hand at the crowded room, her extended nails glinting in the fluorescent light. "Next year we're *seniors*. Then what? We'll be gone too."

Darcy's insides sank. It was as if Tarah's words shook the cafeteria. So many choices were ahead of them. So much unknown.

But it's still far off, right? Darcy tried to convince herself.

"That's why this party is a big deal," Tarah continued. "Coop's gonna be eighteen. With everything that happened this summer . . ." Tarah took a heavy breath. Her eyes almost seemed to glisten. "He's always been there for me, for all of us. Seems like we should be there for him. It's more important than work."

"Tarah, you know I want to be there. I really do," Hakeem explained. "But I can't. If I don't work that weekend, I'll lose the job. I'm sorry." He sounded as miserable as he looked.

Tarah shook her head.

"Fine. Do what you gotta do, then," she said, turning away from him. She reached out and grabbed Darcy's bicep. "Girl, I hope you got some muscles in there," she joked, instantly sounding like her old cheerful self. "We're gonna need 'em, 'cause it looks like you and me are the setup crew!"

"Don't forget about Dez. He'll be there too," Hakeem added. "He's excited to help, and he's almost as big as me."

Desmond, Cooper's younger brother, was a freshman at Bluford. He was also Darcy's sister's boyfriend until two weeks ago.

"Don't worry, Tarah," Darcy assured her, rubbing her friend's back. "We got this!"

"Okay. But since Hakeem's not coming, let's start earlier. Like at two instead of—"

Suddenly, Tarah's grip on Darcy's arm tightened. Her fingers dug into Darcy's skin like claws.

"Ouch!" Darcy snapped.

"Shh! Here he comes!" Tarah's voice dropped to a dramatic whisper. "Act normal!"

Tarah bounded from her seat, meeting Cooper as he emerged from the check-out line in a *Bluford Football* hoodie and jeans. He carried a full tray in his muscular arms. For a second, he eyed Tarah protectively, as if he was concerned about her. But then she whispered something, put a hand on her ample hip, and flashed her manicured nails in his face. Whatever she said made Cooper smile, and Darcy felt a familiar twinge of jealousy. Their relationship looked so comfortable and so easy compared to . . . .

"I'm sorry about this afternoon, Darcy," Hakeem said quietly.

"I'm sorry too," Darcy began. "I wasn't being fair."

"But you were right. Maybe we can see each other tomorrow?" Hakeem suggested.

Darcy shook her head. "I have to tutor."

"Thursday?"

"Scoops."

Hakeem frowned. "What about Sunday? I work until six, but maybe we could meet after?"

"Maybe . . . but I have a chemistry lab due for Ms. Allen." Darcy stared at her notebook rather than looking into Hakeem's face.

"Then we'll have to make time somehow." Hakeem's voice was soft but insistent, just above a whisper. "There's something I want to talk to you about face to face. No texting. Something important."

Just then, Cooper arrived at the table, slapping his plastic tray down as he sat. He grabbed several French fries and shoved them into his mouth. "Want some?" he mumbled between bites.

But Darcy barely heard him. The roar of the cafeteria seemed to fade. The oily scent of the fries hardly registered.

What did Hakeem want to say? Darcy wondered. Was it good news, or was it like the time he told her about Anika, the girl he had met in Detroit?

"Maybe tonight?" she began, trying not to sound desperate. "After you're done at the theater? We can—"

"Darcy Wills, please report to the main office. Darcy Wills to the main office!"

The distorted voice of Bluford High School's secretary, Ms. Bader, crackled through the school's public address system. The noisy cafeteria hushed slightly as students lowered their voices to listen. Again the secretary droned robotically overhead.

"Darcy Wills, please report to the main office. Darcy Wills to the main office, please!"

"Ooooo," moaned someone nearby as if Darcy were in trouble.

"Uh oh, what'd you do, Darcy? Too much homework?" Cooper joked from the other side of the table, a playful grin stretched across his face. "You best watch out if Darth Bader wants you." He quickly pulled up his hood and gave a slow menacing breath that sounded like the movie villain.

"Darcy Wills," Cooper boomed with fake seriousness. He raised an arm as if aiming an invisible force at her. "I find your perfect grades disturbing. Please report to Lord Bader—"

"Stop playin', Coop!" Tarah scolded, swatting at him before he could finish. "This could be serious. What about your mom, Darcy?"

Mom.

The word echoed in Darcy's mind. Tarah was right to be concerned. Her mother, Mattie Wills, was five months pregnant. It had already been a tough pregnancy. Mom had been feeling so tired lately that she had dropped one of her shifts as an ER nurse, something she never did, not even when Grandma had grown sick and frail.

What if something is wrong? Darcy wondered, her pulse suddenly pounding in her temples.

"Darcy Wills, please report to the office. Darcy Wills to the office, please!" The voice called out again. Somehow it seemed more urgent this time. Alarmed, Darcy stood up to leave.

"I'm goin' with you," Hakeem volunteered.

"No," Darcy shook her head. "You need to go to class—"

"I'll walk you down," Tarah said, putting her arm on Darcy's shoulder as if she was unsteady and needed support. "Come on—"

"I'm okay," Darcy said, nudging free of Tarah. "It's probably nothing." Darcy snatched up her book bag and tried to hide the nervous trembling of her fingers. "I'll text you if it's anything."

Darcy rushed from the cafeteria, fear clawing at her with invisible fingers.

Chapter 2

"There you are," Ms. Bader grunted from her massive desk in the back corner of Bluford's main office as Darcy arrived. The room hummed with the electric buzz of fluorescent lights and smelled vaguely of hand sanitizer. "You're to go straight to Ms. Briggs," the secretary barked, barely looking up from her computer.

"Ms. Briggs?" Darcy asked, confused. She had not expected to hear her guidance counselor's name. A bored-looking student in a nearby visitor chair picked his nails and listened, a scowl on his face.

"Yes. Go on, she's waiting for you. And no, *you're* not in trouble," the secretary added, glancing sternly at the student. "Ms. Spencer is ready for you now, Tyray."

Darcy grabbed a hall pass and made the short walk to the guidance office.

Sandwiched between the main office and the gym, the guidance office was lined with glass panels that faced the hall-way, allowing students to see into it as they passed by. Colorful flyers and moti-vational posters were taped to many of the panels.

The Future Depends on What You Do Today, read one of them.

"No, the future is just another f-word." Darcy recalled what Tarah had said about the poster a few weeks ago. They had laughed at the time, but now for some reason it seemed less funny.

The guidance office was eerily quiet when Darcy stepped inside. An aging speckled carpet covered the floor and blocked most of the sound from the hall. A cluster of saggy maroon-cushioned chairs formed an L-shaped waiting area for guests. Opposite them, a narrow corridor led back to a series of small offices for Bluford's counselors. Between the offices and the waiting area, a wooden work table, nicked and gouged with years of use, held a display of college brochures and a few books about preparing for the SAT. A famil-iar student sat at the table reading them: Brisana Meeks.

Darcy nearly tripped when she saw her.

"Good. You're both here," a voice called out before Darcy could say anything.

Ms. Briggs, a plump, light-skinned woman with dyed red hair, burst from the first tiny office. Darcy had met with her twice since starting at Bluford. Both times, like today, Ms. Briggs had worn a tangle of bracelets that made a metallic clinking sound whenever her hands moved, which was constantly.

"Come," she urged. The clinking punctuated her words as she waved both girls into her cramped office. "Sit down."

Darcy followed Brisana and grabbed a chair in front of a row of steel file cabinets. Stacks of folders, some thick and others thin, crowded the computer on Ms. Briggs's desk. A large poster hung on the wall with giant hand-sized text that seemed to scream at anyone in the room.

What You Say in Here Stays in Here, it read.

Darcy wondered how many students stared at that poster and what they might have told Ms. Briggs.

She doubted the counselor could find anything in her cluttered office, but then she noticed a slender file with her name on it resting under the counselor's hand. A folder with Brisana's name was there, too.

"I bet you're wondering why I called you in," Ms. Briggs said as she scooted her chair toward them, a tight-lipped smile on her face.

"Yes, ma'am," Brisana said in the sweet voice she reserved for adults. Darcy had heard it countless times. They had been friends since grade school, but that changed last year when Darcy and Tarah became close. Since then, Brisana had been icy and mean at times, always trying to convince Darcy that Tarah was no good.

"*A zero*," Brisana had called her.

Once, Brisana even tried to come between her and Hakeem. The episode would have destroyed their relationship if Tarah hadn't convinced Darcy to give Brisana a second chance. Despite perfect grades, flawless coppery skin, stylish clothes, and her sometimes snobby attitude, Brisana was troubled. Her distracted parents didn't seem to notice or care. In July, when Brisana got into a relationship with an older boy who broke her heart and left her fearful she might be pregnant, she had turned to Darcy for help, not her parents. Tarah had quietly helped Darcy get Brisana to a doctor—an experience Darcy would never forget, especially the sound of Brisana sobbing in relief and sadness at the ordeal. It was a side of Brisana no one knew, one Darcy was certain Ms. Briggs never imagined.

"Well, I won't keep you in suspense any longer," the counselor said, shattering the memory. "I have some wonderful news." She paused dramatically. "You know Trinity College, right?"

Brisana's eyes widened. Darcy recognized the name. It was a small private college outside the city where wealthy kids went to school.

"Well, *yeah*," Brisana spoke is if Ms. Briggs had just asked a dumb question. "Who doesn't know about Trinity?"

"Of course. I forgot who I was talking to," Ms. Briggs said with a knowing smile. "But here's something you may not know. Every year, two high-achieving juniors from each of the city's public high schools are selected for Trinity's Bridge Program. It's reserved for juniors who demonstrate real academic potential. I'm happy to say you two were chosen from Bluford!"

"Oh my God!" Brisana cheered, her face beaming.

Ms. Briggs handed them each a slick, glossy folder. The cover showed a group of fresh-faced teenagers of different complexions stepping purposefully on a footbridge.

A handsome tree-lined campus dotted with important-looking buildings stretched before them.

The words *Bridge to Excellence* glowed in striking letters across the top of the folder. Beneath them in smaller script was a second line.

Infinite Possibilities Await.

"This is awesome!" Brisana cheered. She hugged the folder to her chest and danced in her seat, her braids swinging around her chin as she shimmied and nudged Darcy. "Isn't this amazing, Darcy? We made it!"

"Wow . . . I mean . . . just, wow." Darcy stammered, struggling to absorb the news. "I'm surprised. I remember filling out a form when we took the PSAT, but I never thought—"

"Well, you did it! Congratulations, both of you," Ms. Briggs said, with a grin so wide her cheeks looked as if they might burst. "I just got the packet and couldn't wait to tell you the news."

Darcy smiled and tried to look excited. But in Ms. Briggs's intense stare, she felt pressured somehow, especially because Brisana was so happy.

"Are you familiar with how the program works?" Ms. Briggs asked, her bracelets jingling slightly as she flipped through the paperwork from Trinity College.

"Oh yes! I remember reading about the program," Brisana gushed, still in her teacher's pet voice. Darcy hadn't seen her this excited in years. "We meet in small groups with other Bridge students each month during the school year."

"That's right," Ms. Briggs said nodding in approval.

"Really?" Darcy asked. She had barely paid attention to the paperwork from Trinity College when she took the PSAT.

"Here's the best part," Brisana added. "Next summer, we get to spend two weeks on campus, staying in a dorm and taking some classes so we're ready for college work."

Ms. Briggs laughed. "Brisana, you *have* been doing your homework! You got it just right. It's one of the best programs I know. Even if you don't go to Trinity for college, you get valuable experience about what college is like. And guess what else: It's completely free!"

Darcy's heart skipped in her chest. On one hand, the news was great. She knew she should be thrilled, and part of her was. But another part felt bothered. She was barely a junior, and now a college she didn't choose was forcing her to face a future she wasn't ready for. The trees, footbridge, and chiseled buildings were a different world from Bluford High School. An alien planet.

Do I want this? a voice inside her said.

But then in a flash, she pictured herself on Trinity's campus walking with the attractive, fresh-faced kids on the brochure. She imagined herself being in class with them, being as smart as them. Maybe being smarter.

Infinite possibilities, the words on the brochure sang out to her.

Could I really go there? she wondered. *Maybe Hakeem could go to school there too.* The idea played in her mind like a movie. He could study music. They would graduate together, find jobs, and get a house surrounded by green grass instead of the dry, trash-strewn patches in their neighborhood.

Maybe my parents could stay with us.

Maybe Mom wouldn't have to work so hard.

Maybe the baby could play outside in the yard.

Darcy let the images spool in slow motion in her mind, especially the part of her walking hand in hand on campus with Hakeem . . .

"But," Ms. Briggs's voice sliced through Darcy's fantasy. "They've done it again."

"Done what?" Brisana asked.

"They sent out the acceptance notices late. They always do," She sighed. "You have to decide immediately. Orientation is next Saturday and you must be there or you could lose your spot." She raised a finger at Darcy and Brisana, making her bracelets *ting* like cymbals in a tiny marching band. "I hope that won't be a problem."

Next Saturday? The date snagged in her mind for a second, and then she realized why: *Cooper's surprise party.* Darcy gulped.

Tarah nearly had a meltdown when Hakeem told her he couldn't make it. Darcy knew there was no way she could miss it. Tarah would never forgive her. Darcy flipped the brochure to its back. In a red circle she saw the time of the orientation: *10 a.m. until 2 p.m.*

"I'll be there!" Brisana assured her.

"Excellent," Ms. Briggs said, turning to Darcy with her eyebrows raised in question. "How about you? You can make it, right?"

"I-I'll try," Darcy stammered.

"*Try?* Do you have a conflict? Is it work?"

"No, it's nothing like that—"

21

"Then what is it?" Ms. Briggs leaned forward. The smile left her face.

"I'm supposed to help a friend with something."

Ms. Briggs frowned. "Darcy, do you know how important this is? There are hundreds of kids in this city who would jump at this opportunity. Most will never get the chance. Don't give Trinity College reason to doubt you. Adjust your schedule. You need to be there."

"I will, Ms. Briggs," Darcy assured her, trying to sound convincing.

"I hope so." The counselor dropped her gaze and pointed to Darcy's folder. "Oh, and another thing: A parent or guardian must accompany you to the orientation. Directions and permission forms are in your packets. Get them signed and bring them with you. Understand?"

Darcy nodded as Brisana grinned and shimmied in her seat. Ms. Briggs stepped around her desk and gave them each a quick hug. "Congratulations to you both, ladies. You will make Bluford proud. This is a big deal, girls. A *very* big deal."

"Is *that* it?" Tarah scoffed at the end of the day, flipping over the Trinity College brochure Darcy just handed her.

"That's it."

"They had me scared half to death. I thought something was *wrong*. I mean, you never get called to the office." Tarah glanced at the students on the footbridge and handed it right back. "Whatever. Where's Coop at?" she asked, craning her neck at the stream of students leaving the school. "He better not be late."

The afternoon had gone by in a blur. Darcy could barely remember what they had talked about in English or the organic molecules they had reviewed in chemistry. Something about carboxyl groups? What she did recall was reading the Trinity Bridge Program brochure several times.

Could I really go there?

Could I live there for two weeks next summer?

What'll happen when I'm gone?

Darcy couldn't stop the questions. The longest she had ever been away from home was a week, and even that was a decade ago when Grandma was still alive and healthy and had her small home on the other side of the city. A lifetime ago.

This would be different. New places and new people.

Infinite possibilities.

The thought scared her, but it also made her palms tingle with excitement—until she pictured Tarah's reaction to the news that she would miss setting up for Cooper's party. She knew she had to tell Tarah as soon as possible.

"It looks like a great program though, right?" Darcy began nervously. "I mean it's not something I can pass up—"

"Uh huh," Tarah said absently, grabbing her phone and scrolling through a seemingly endless stream of messages. She paused to scan the crowd of students exiting the school.

"But there's this orientation," Darcy continued, choosing her words carefully. "Ms. Briggs got late notice about it and—"

"Where is that boy?" Tarah put a hand on her hip and shook her head in frustration. "Honestly . . ."

"All of us have to be there, or we could lose our spots." Darcy leaned slightly closer to Tarah, looking for some evidence that her words were being heard. "I think it can work if we just—"

"Darcy!" A grating singsongy voice sliced through the air.

Darcy turned to see Brisana sauntering over to where they stood, a grin on her face that dimmed slightly when she and

Tarah locked eyes. "Hey, Tarah," she added coolly, sizing up Tarah's jeans and the lip of belly fat straining against her red top. "Did Darcy tell you our news about Trinity College?"

"Yeah, she told me," Tarah replied, sounding bored. She scanned her phone again. "You see Cooper inside?"

Brisana shook her head at his name, as if Tarah mentioned a disease she didn't want to catch. Tarah's thumbs moved across her phone in a blur, her eyes glued to her screen.

"Are you walking home, Darcy?" Brisana asked, wedging herself so that she was almost between Darcy and Tarah. "We need to talk. Did you read the whole brochure? The group we meet next Saturday is the one we'll be with the entire year—"

"Hold up." Tarah hands sliced through the air as if she were suddenly directing traffic. "Did she say next *Saturday*? What's she talking about? Please tell me she got her days wrong."

"That's what I was trying to tell you!" Darcy said, clutching her books to her chest like a shield as she backed away from Tarah slightly. "That's the day of our orientation."

"You're skippin' it, right?" Tarah demanded. "Didn't you tell them you had plans?"

"I did. But if I miss this, I could lose my spot—"

"Your *spot*?!" Tarah eyes flashed with anger and hurt. "You promised you'd be there, Darcy. I *need* your help with all the—"

"Here he comes," Brisana cut in, seeming almost as bored as Tarah had been only minutes earlier.

Darcy spotted Cooper exiting through the high school's main doors. She lowered her voice and tried to explain.

"Tarah, the orientation ends early. I'll still be there, I promise."

Tarah scowled. For a split second, her jaw dropped as if she was about to yell, but then she stopped herself.

"You ready, Tarah?" Cooper weaved through the thinning crowd, his bright eyes darting between Darcy and Tarah as if he saw something that concerned him. "Everything good?"

"Yeah, we cool," Tarah said icily.

"Yeah!" Darcy added, trying to sound normal. "Everything's fine, Coop."

Cooper slipped his arm around Tarah, but she didn't budge. She was still staring intently at Darcy, who saw disappointment and something else in Tarah's eyes. Several seconds passed in agonizing silence.

"C'mon, T," Cooper said. "We don't want to be late."

"Yeah, we don't want to lose our *spot*," Tarah huffed, breaking her stare with Darcy.

"Where you two going?" Brisana asked, suddenly curious.

"Nowhere special," Tarah answered quickly. "Go on to the truck, Coop. I'll be right there. I need to talk to Darcy for a minute more. Privately."

"You sure?" Cooper asked. "Don't make me late or I'ma go Ms. Bader on you and give you a Saturday detention."

Tarah shoved him away with mock irritation. "Make *you* late? After all the time I spend waitin' on you, you owe me a month of Saturdays," she huffed, nudging him aside.

"I'm leaving," Brisana said, rolling her eyes. "Text me later, Darcy."

"She don't need to," Tarah cut in, not even looking at Brisana. "I'll only be a second. You can wait."

Darcy watched as Cooper crossed the street to his old truck. She wished she could calm Tarah, assure her somehow, but she didn't know what to say. "Look Tarah, I'm sorry—"

"You promise you'll be there by three?" Tarah cut her off.

"Definitely," Darcy vowed. "Where else am I gonna be?"

"All right, then." Tarah's face softened. "I'm not gonna lie. I need you, girl. With everything me and Coop been through lately, it's been stressful . . ." she took a deep breath. "Dez and Roylin are gonna help, but I want this done right. You're the only one I trust for that."

Tarah suddenly seemed serious—too serious, as if their conversation was about more than Cooper's party. Darcy wanted to ask, but Cooper was waiting. She could see him in his truck shaking his head.

"Don't worry. The orientation ends at 2 p.m. It's only an hour away. I'll be there by three," Darcy insisted. "We'll get everything done before he shows up. We *got* this, Tarah."

Tarah nodded, seeming relieved.

"I hope so, girl. I'm hoping we can catch up too."

"Me too!" Darcy replied.

Cooper's horn blasted from across the street.

"C'mon, Tarah, we're gonna be late!" he yelled.

Tarah closed her eyes and took a deep breath.

Was she okay? Darcy wondered.

"I gotta go, Darce. Congratulations on your college thing," Tarah muttered, hurrying to Cooper's truck. A second later, they raced off in a cloud of noise and exhaust.

"Where you think they're going?" Brisana asked, as the truck disappeared in traffic.

"I have no idea."

"Don't take this wrong, but why are you even going to that party?"

"Can you stop for once!" Darcy snapped. "I'm going because they're my friends. Maybe if you were nicer, you'd have more."

"Seriously, Darcy, you don't need friends like that. You need to start thinking about your future," Brisana said.

"Is this what you want to talk about? Because if it is, I'm done with this conversation."

"Look!" Brisana said, holding the brochure up in Darcy's face. The words *Bridge to Excellence* screamed from the page. "Say what you want, but Tarah's people aren't *these* people. None of them are going to college. If you don't watch out, they're gonna drag you down."

"You don't know anything about her! Tarah wouldn't drag anyone down. She's always there for me. She was even there for you, remember?"

"You sure about that?" Brisana challenged, ignoring Darcy's question.

"What do you mean?"

"Look what just happened. Tarah didn't care about your news. I'm not saying she's a bad person. But she doesn't get *this* the way you and I do," Brisana said, clutching the brochure.

Darcy had heard Brisana put down Tarah many times. Usually she was petty and easy to ignore. But this was different. For some reason, her words were sticky in Darcy's mind, clinging to her thoughts even though Darcy didn't want them to.

"You got her all wrong, Brisana," Darcy insisted. "She's one of the smartest people I know. And she's real. She's got a future, too—"

"Really? Doing what? Her nails?" Brisana shot back.

"That's it. I'm done with this," Darcy snapped.

"No you're *not* done. You're just getting started. We both are—and that's my point," Brisana shot back, stepping in Darcy's path. "I get that you like her, but we're juniors now, Darcy. *Juniors*. Things are about to get real. We've got big choices to make. And Tarah won't help you make them. You're headed one way, and she's headed another. How long do you think you can stay friends when you don't have anything in common?"

"You know who has nothing in common? Us!" Darcy fumed, shouldering past Brisana.

"You know I'm right," Brisana added. "You just don't want to admit it."

Darcy stormed off, unable to silence the ugly words Brisana planted in her mind.

Chapter 3

"Saturday?!" Mom roared that night when Darcy announced the news about Trinity College. "Next week? That's impossible. We can't do it."

"What?!" Darcy exclaimed, stunned at her mother's response.

"We're proud of you, Darcy. We really are. But we can't drop everything right now and go to that informational meeting, not on such short notice," Mom explained as she rubbed her temples.

Darcy couldn't believe her ears. She knew Cooper's party was an obstacle to the orientation program, but she figured her parents would be happy and supportive. Instead, they acted as if the news bothered them.

"But if I miss the orientation, I'm out!" Darcy groaned. "They'll give my spot to someone else! We're the only ones from Bluford who were chosen!"

Darcy's father leaned forward in his chair at the kitchen table, his elbows bent, his hands knotted under his chin. Dressed in the charcoal jacket and slate baseball cap he wore on nights he worked as an Uber driver, he looked old to Darcy. Gone was the youthful man with coffee skin, jet black hair, and playful eyes who used to carry her on his back and make up corny stories to make her laugh. That man abandoned them for another woman years ago. When he finally returned last year, sad and contrite, he had transformed. His skin had grown saggy and weathered, his eyes darker and more somber. Darcy saw how hard he worked to rebuild trust since he had come back into their lives, and it showed on his face. Creases lined his once smooth cheeks, and his hair, now mixed with spots of silver, had receded slightly.

Lately, Darcy noticed the years were showing on Mom, too. Puffy circles hung under her eyes no matter how much sleep she got, and she complained constantly of sore feet and an aching back. She slouched in the chair next to Dad, her black maternity pants stretched tight over the baby bump where her hands rested.

"I don't know. Maybe you could go by yourself if we could find a way to get you there," Mom suggested, flipping through the Trinity College folder.

Darcy explained how Ms. Briggs said a parent or guardian needed to attend. "I don't understand. Why can't one of you go? You're always driving Jamee places."

"That's not fair, Darcy. And it's not true either."

"Yeah, why are you even bringing me into this?" yelled Jamee, Darcy's younger sister, from her nearby bedroom.

"I'm sorry, Darcy," Mom said, ignoring Jamee's question. "But we have something important we have to do next Saturday."

"Important? You mean this isn't important—"

"Tell her why we can't go, Mattie," Dad cut in. His voice sounded hoarse, as if he had been talking for hours. "She deserves to know. They both do."

"What is it?" Darcy asked. "Is something wrong?"

Her parents stared at each other. Mom inhaled deeply and sighed. Jamee emerged from her bedroom.

"What's going on?" she asked.

Had Dad been drinking again? Darcy wondered. Had they been fighting? A flood of worries spilled through Darcy's mind before Mom finally spoke up.

"We have an appointment with a doctor on Saturday—"

"*A doctor?*"

"Yes. We spent the whole afternoon arranging it so we could both go. Dad's missing work. I'm missing a shift at the hospital. They're squeezing us in on short notice with a specialist. I'm sorry, but we have to do this."

"But why?" Darcy asked, struggling to make sense of what her parents were saying.

"Yeah. Is something wrong?" Jamee shut off her phone and sat at the table.

"I'm old," Mom answered with a sad laugh.

"You're not old."

"To be having a baby, I am," Mom explained. "I'm much older than I was when I had you girls. For people my age, pregnancy can be complicated. So I have to get all these extra tests—"

"*Tests?*"

"Just to make sure everything's okay," Dad answered quickly. His words seemed forced. "They do them for older mothers

35

as a precaution. Nothing to worry about," he added, almost as if he were trying to convince himself.

"But since I'm not allowed to drive after the tests, your father needs to take me. The good news is we'll find out if the baby is a boy or girl. But the bad news is we won't be able to take you to the orientation. If it were anything else, we'd cancel it to be there," Mom insisted.

"Both of us would," Dad added, rubbing his neck as if it were strained.

Darcy felt a twinge of guilt for being so upset. Their news made the orientation seem silly and unimportant. Mom was right to look out for the baby, Darcy's little sister or brother. The idea still felt strange, even though Mom announced the pregnancy months ago.

"I'm sorry. I didn't know. I'll tell Ms. Briggs."

"No. *I'll* call her," Mom grumbled. "I don't care how special they think they are. Life is messy. I work in an ER and see it every day. They need to allow us to reschedule, or let you go alone."

Messy.

The word echoed in Darcy's mind as she glanced at the brochure. The faces on the cover beamed back at her with perfect smiles, perfect teeth, perfect skin. They seemed to come from a planet where messiness didn't exist, where Dads didn't leave their families, grandparents never got sick, and kids never had to care for them or say goodbye forever.

All we got is messy, Darcy thought to herself, remembering her grandmother and how she had died in her sleep in the bedroom down the hall. It happened just last summer, though it felt much longer.

If Grandma were here and still strong, she'd take me to Trinity College. Darcy was certain of it. She wished she could tell Grandma the news that she had been accepted into the program.

I'm so proud of you, Angelcake, Darcy could almost hear her say.

"Maybe there's another way," Dad spoke up, interrupting Darcy's thoughts.

"There's isn't, Carl. You know what the doctor said. We can't skip—"

"Charlotte," Dad said. The name seemed to suck the air out of the kitchen. Mom's face flinched for a second as if she smelled something unpleasant, but then her eyes widened. "Do you think she could take Darcy?"

"Are you serious?" Jamee exclaimed. "Oh, I am so glad this doesn't involve me."

Aunt Charlotte. Darcy hadn't even considered it. The idea of visiting Trinity College with her stuffy aunt seemed as foreign as the college itself. Darcy's aunt lived in a fancy townhouse on the other end of town. She worked at a bank and made lots of money, which she was never afraid to flaunt with her clothes, her car, or the expensive trips she took. Though she and Mom were sisters, they didn't agree on much. By far, the biggest issue with Aunt Charlotte was how she had treated Grandma after her stroke. Aunt Charlotte had wanted to put her in a nursing home, but Mom insisted on caring for her at home. The disagreement caused a wound in the family that still hadn't healed.

"There's only one way to find out," Mom said, grabbing her phone. She stared at it for a few seconds as if she dreaded the call she was about to make. The swell of her belly seemed larger than ever.

"It's okay, Mom," Darcy began. "Don't call her—"

"No, it's not okay. There's no reason you should miss out because we have to go to the doctor. Besides, Charlotte's always been interested in helping you girls succeed. Remember how she once talked about taking you to France? She might be excited to do this with you."

"I don't care where I need to go," Jamee mumbled, "Aunt Charlotte is *not* taking me."

"And don't let her cook for you either!" Dad joked. The one thing everyone agreed about Aunt Charlotte was that her home-cooked meals were horrible. "Remember that eggplant casserole?"

"Yuck!" Jamee exclaimed. Mom smiled weakly but also waved for them to be quiet as she made the phone call.

"Hello, Charlotte?" Mom's voice sounded forced at first, but quickly eased. Darcy listened as her mother described the Bridge Program and the weekend orientation. She was just about to ask the question, Darcy could tell, when Aunt Charlotte said something that stopped her.

"I can't go because I have some tests to take . . . medical tests," she said, lowering her voice. She got up from the table and darted to her bedroom. When she emerged ten minutes later, Mom looked as if she had eaten one of Aunt Charlotte's home-made stews.

"Okay, that's done. Charlotte will take you. Problem solved," Mom said, rubbing her shoulder wearily and looking back toward her room. "But after that conversation, I need a nap," she announced.

"And I gotta go." Dad stood up, adjusting his hat. "Since I'm out next Saturday, I need to pick up all the rides I can. I'll be working the airport tonight." He gave Mom a quick kiss on the cheek and gently rubbed her belly. "It's gonna be all right," he whispered as he left.

But Darcy saw something lurking in his eyes. Concern or maybe something more: fear. She wondered if Jamee noticed it too, but her sister's face was locked on her phone, her thumbs moving in a blur on the screen. For a split second, Darcy thought she saw a picture of students in Bluford's locker room, but when she leaned in for a better look, Jamee pocketed her phone.

"I got homework," she said abruptly and rushed down the hallway.

Mom waddled to her bedroom and closed the door, leaving Darcy alone in the suddenly quiet kitchen, her mind buzzing with questions.

College. Hakeem. Tarah.

And now something else: her parents. The baby. Was something wrong? Were they hiding something serious?

*   *   *

Can u meet? Playground. 20 min?

Hakeem's text arrived after Darcy finished her Thursday shift at Scoops, the ice cream shop where she had worked part time since the summer. She and Jamee had just eaten dinner. Jamee fled to her room after the meal, leaving a ketchup-smeared plate on the table as if Darcy were her maid.

"I cooked. You're supposed to do the dishes," Darcy hollered through Jamee's closed bedroom door.

"I *know*," Jamee yelled. "I'll do it later."

"That's what you always say," Darcy grumbled. "I'm not covering for you this time. If Mom sees it—"

"I *said* I'll do it later!" Jamee repeated, yanking open the door and glaring at Darcy. "You're not Mom. You don't have to nag me! Besides, if you do this college thing next summer, I'm going to have to do everything myself around here," she huffed.

"Good. For once you'll know how I feel!" Darcy snapped. She pictured Jamee cooking, scrubbing, folding, and shopping while Darcy strolled the leafy campus of

41

Trinity College. The thought almost made her smile as Jamee shut her bedroom door.

Darcy quickly answered Hakeem's text. *OMW*, she wrote and got ready to leave.

She was rushing toward the front door when her phone began vibrating. Darcy was so sure it was Hakeem, she didn't check the number before answering.

"Did you get my text? I'm on my way," she said.

"You're coming here?" an unexpected voice replied. It was Tarah.

"Oh, no . . ." Darcy laughed. "I thought you were Hak—"

Tarah cut in before Darcy could explain.

"You think Jamee could come over early Saturday to help? You know, with setting up for Coop's party? Since you're doing your college thing and won't be there until three."

Tarah's words hung like an off-key note in a church choir.

Darcy felt her eyes twitch in annoyance. Tarah made it seem as though she had chosen something small and silly over Cooper's party. Tarah didn't seem to care if the program could impact Darcy's future. And she didn't seem to care about Jamee, either.

"I don't know, Tarah . . ." Darcy said slowly, swallowing back her irritation.

42

"You really think it's a good idea to put her and Dez together right now?" she asked.

Jamee and Desmond were a couple until just two weeks ago. They broke up after someone spread rumors in school that Jamee hooked up with a girl on the cheerleading team. The stories were false, but for a short time, Dez believed them and confronted Jamee. She never forgave him for doubting her or reacting the way he did.

"Remember the whole thing with that girl Angel?"

"Oh, yeah," Tarah replied, her voice limp and distracted. "Right. I forgot about that."

Forgot?! Darcy nearly dropped her phone. It didn't seem possible that Tarah of all people could forget that. Until now, Tarah had always been the person who remembered details and could figure out why someone might be upset. It was one reason Darcy liked Tarah so much.

"I mean, do you even need the extra help, Tarah?" Darcy asked, trying to hide what she really felt—that Tarah's obsessing over the party was becoming a problem. "Cooper won't get there until six, so we'll have three full hours. You've thrown bigger parties than this. That reunion you

43

did last summer was, like, twice as big, right?"

"You mean the one you didn't go to?" Tarah snapped.

Darcy winced. She realized she should not have mentioned it. Yes, she had missed Tarah's family reunion, but why was it such a big deal? It was a family event with a bunch of Tarah's relatives, not a friends party. Still, Tarah remained angry about it and brought it up whenever she had the chance.

"Tarah, I'm sorry, okay? How many times do I have to say it? I had to work!"

"Always somethin' right?" Tarah said, ignoring the apology. "Anyway, this is different. This one's for Coop. Don't you understand? It needs to be perfect—"

"It will be, Tarah. Besides, it's Cooper. He'd be happy with pizza and soda!"

"But *I* won't," Tarah declared, her voice rising. "I mean, I know it's not your college thing, but it's important to me!"

There it was again: *your college thing*.

This time, the words hit like a slap. Darcy blinked in surprise. Tarah had teased her before. Last year, she had even accused Darcy of acting as if she was smarter than everyone else. But that was a long time ago. They had grown to be close friends since then—at least that's what Darcy thought. But now something was changing. Tarah seemed to be trying to hurt her or push her away. Why? Confusion and anger bubbled in Darcy's chest.

"What's wrong, Tarah?" she asked carefully. "Did I do something—"

"No, forget it. Just ask Jamee if she'll come early. Text me what she says," Tarah said tersely. "I gotta go." Tarah hung up before Darcy could ask another question.

Annoyed, Darcy shoved the phone in her pocket and stomped down the hall to Jamee's room, knocking twice on the closed door.

"What?" her sister yelled. "I told you I'll do the dishes later!"

Darcy pushed the door open and poked her head inside. Clothes, papers, random shoes, and an empty soda can were strewn about as if a small tornado had just swept through. Mom used to bug Jamee about cleaning her room, but that stopped when Mom announced she was pregnant. Now, as long as Jamee's door was closed and the mess didn't spill into the hall, Mom didn't say a word. To Darcy, it seemed there were two sets of rules: strict ones for her and a looser set for Jamee. And yet it was always Jamee who complained things were unfair.

"What do you want?" Jamee asked. She sprawled on her cluttered bed with her phone in hand, one eye on the small screen and the other on Darcy. The stack of laundry Darcy folded yesterday had toppled over, spilling clean clothes on the dirty carpet.

"Great!" Darcy yelled in annoyance. "I spent half an hour folding that stuff for you and now it's on the floor!"

Jamee rolled her eyes and tossed her phone aside. "What do you want?" she repeated.

"I'm going out," Darcy said bluntly. "In case you need me, I'll be back in an hour."

"Where you goin'?" Jamee sat up, her brown eyes suddenly bright with curiosity.

"The playground."

Jamee wrinkled her nose. "Why would you hang around there? Too many little kids."

"None of your business."

"You're meeting Hakeem, aren't you?"

When Darcy nodded, Jamee smiled as if she had just won an argument.

"Are you finally going to have *the talk*?"

"What talk?"

"You know. The one that makes it official. That you're back. A couple again. I mean that's what you're doing, right?"

"OK, I'm leaving," Darcy said, shutting down Jamee's questions. "I don't need relationship advice from my little sister."

"Even if it's right?" Jamee asked. Her phone pinged as if she had just scored a point. "Oh, it's Amberlynn. It's about time." Again Jamee's fingers flashed across her screen, and she seemed to forget Darcy was there.

"Bye, Jamee," Darcy said finally, leaving the house. She decided not to mention Tarah's request. After everything Tarah said, Darcy didn't feel like doing her any favors.

Chapter 4

The late-afternoon sun bathed apart-
ments and storefronts in fiery orange as
Darcy made her way to the park to meet
Hakeem. Fading graffiti, like old tattoos,
covered the low cement wall that surrounded the park, all of it familiar to Darcy.

She eased through a gap in the wall
as she had done countless times before. A
new work of graffiti, a black sphere with
a lit fuse, had been painted near the first
swing set. Underneath the sphere, crude
jagged letters spelled out a single word.
Timebomb.

As Darcy moved further into the park,
the sounds of the neighborhood grew more
distant. The roar of passing traffic, the
thudding bass of reggaeton music from a
nearby apartment, even the *chop chop* of a
police helicopter, became muted.

She spotted Hakeem rocking gently back and forth on a swing. He stood up as soon as he saw her, and Darcy felt her heartbeat skip and quicken as their eyes met. He was growing his hair a bit longer and it only made him even more handsome. More mature.

"Hey," he said, smiling and rubbing his hands against his jeans as if he were nervous. "You want to talk here or go somewhere else?"

"Here's good," Darcy said, taking a seat on the swing. Hakeem sat down beside her.

They stared out over the playground in silence. Darcy recalled how last year Tarah, Cooper, and Hakeem had joined a group of Bluford students to clean up the park. They had spent an entire Saturday removing trash, repainting the seesaws, sweeping up broken bottles, and even washing away some of the graffiti. When Darcy heard what they had done, she was impressed.

"There is no way I'm spending Saturday cleaning up other people's trash," Brisana groaned at the time, but that was when Darcy began noticing Hakeem. Really noticing him.

"Excuse me," a tiny voice called from behind them. "Could I have a turn?"

Darcy turned to see a small boy, maybe five or six years old in a Hulk T-shirt, eyeing the swings.

"It's all yours, little Hulk," Hakeem said with a smile, rising from his swing so the little boy could take it.

"Thank you," said a woman on a nearby bench. "Say thank you, Diego."

Hakeem gave the little boy a fist bump when he thanked him. The whole exchange lasted a few seconds, but it captured everything Darcy liked about Hakeem. He was unlike any boy she had known: strong but gentle and kind, too. He was the opposite of Brian Mason, the guy she had kissed last summer who wanted to go further and didn't want to take no for an answer. Darcy's father intervened, but the ordeal scarred her. It was a nightmare she had worked hard to forget. Hakeem helped, even now as he said goodbye to Diego.

"Oh my God," Darcy said, unable to contain her smile. "You're so cute with that little boy."

"He's the Hulk," Hakeem joked, his dark eyes sparkling. "You gotta treat the Hulk with respect."

"I've done plenty of babysitting. Let's just say, respect isn't the first thing that comes to mind when dealing with little kids."

"Yeah, but you never babysat the Hulk. C'mon," he urged, walking over to a picnic table and sitting down. Again, he wiped his hands on his jeans. "So I heard about the Trinity program. That's amazing, Darce."

He sounded genuinely happy, the first person who wasn't acting weird or stressed out about the news. But he also seemed to have something else on his mind.

"Thanks. I mean it's exciting and all, but it's kinda surprising," she admitted. "I'm still trying to figure out what it means, you know?"

Hakeem nodded. "What it means is you're crushin' it, Darcy. You're like the athlete who gets picked in the first round of the draft. Don't be surprised. You deserve it. You worked hard to get yours. Talk about respect. I got mad respect for you."

Darcy felt her face flush and her heart flutter. She felt exposed somehow, but safe too. It was as if Hakeem really knew and appreciated her.

"Thanks," she said, leaning toward him slightly. "You deserve it too."

"Nah. I'm a good student, but you and Brisana just killed it. I'm cool, though." He shook his head but also smiled. Darcy

51

could hear the feeling in his words. He meant what he said, but was there sadness too? She wasn't sure.

"Well, you know who's not cool? Tarah. She won't even talk to me about it."

"Don't get me started on her and Coop," Hakeem huffed. "I don't mean to throw shade, but those two right now . . ."

"Really?" Darcy said, surprised to hear Hakeem's reaction. "What is it?"

"You know Coop's my boy, right? If it weren't for him, I wouldn't even be here, so let me say that first. But ever since I got back, things changed between us. We don't talk no more, not for real anyway. It's like something happened this summer, but he won't say what it is."

"Oh my God, that's how Tarah is with me," Darcy confessed. "Did you ask him?"

"He don't wanna talk. All he ever does anymore is hang out with Tarah. He barely leaves her side. It's like he's protecting her or something."

Hakeem sounded defeated. Darcy imagined what it must be like for him to be so far from his family only to have his best friend treating him like a stranger. She wondered why Tarah and Cooper were acting so oddly.

"I thought it was just the party," Darcy admitted. "I figure when that's over, maybe things'll go back to normal—"

"*The party*," Hakeem said, sucking his teeth. "That's another thing. I feel bad enough about missing it without her puttin' me on blast."

"Don't worry," Darcy said, remembering how he had struggled to tell Tarah he couldn't go. "Tarah gets it. She knows you need to work. She's cool with you, but me . . . that's a different story. She has no time for my *college thing*."

Hakeem shook his head and pushed has palms against his legs, straightening his back as if he was forcing away an unpleasant memory. "Hold up. Let's just pause on the two of them for a minute," he said. "I love them both, but I didn't come out here to talk about them."

Darcy noticed Hakeem's voice and face changed as he spoke. He seemed more focused, his eyes intense and sparkling in the fading sun. He took a deep breath, as if he was about to make an important announcement.

"I had a lot of time to think lately. Maybe too much time—I just can't sleep in Casa de Coop," Hakeem said, turning and meeting her gaze. "You and me . . . it's like we never got a chance, you know? And when my dad got sick, and then all the drama of the summer . . . well, it seemed like maybe we never would."

Darcy hung on his words.

You and me.

The chatter of Diego and his mom not far away, the lengthening shadows in the park, a distant siren. None of it mattered. She had never heard Hakeem be so direct. Her heart raced as he continued.

"But I'm b-back. And we're here. And there's no other girl like you, Darcy. Not in the whole s-school. And . . ." he stammered, making a hissing sound like a deflating tire. "Man, this is hard to s-say!" he exclaimed.

"What?" Darcy asked, her heart galloping in her chest.

Hakeem reached into his pocket and pulled out his phone. "I knew this would happen, but like I said, I h-had to time to think. Here's what I'm trying to say."

He tapped the screen, and a video began to play. It opened with Hakeem sitting on a gray chair holding his guitar. The walls around him were wood-paneled, and the ceiling was low, maybe just a few inches above Hakeem's head if he stood. A section of mattress was visible on the floor. His crumpled backpack rested next to it. She knew it had to be his room in Cooper's basement.

Suddenly, Hakeem's hands began to strum, and the guitar chords vibrated through the speakers of his phone. And Hakeem's voice, stronger and more sure, rose above them.

> *Again*
> *No matter the distance or the pain*
> *In blinding sun and pouring rain*
> *When hope was lost, no bridge to cross*
> *Our world gone but feelings remained*
> *And so I ask if you're like me*
> *If you can see what we can be*
> *That we try*
> *You and I*
> *Again*

Darcy felt as if the park had suddenly broken free from the city. The noisy neighborhood was gone, and a private island paradise had taken its place. There were no cramped wood-paneled basements. No parents with secrets and heartache. No friends with hidden drama. No circling police cars.

Just the two of them.

Hakeem shut off his phone and pulled something from his pocket.

"For you," he said, placing a small blue square box in Darcy's palm. She opened it to reveal a heart-shaped gold pendant on a chain. "I got it last year before I knew my dad was sick. I was gonna ask you to wear it and, you know, be my girl," he finished quickly. "It never happened, but I'm thinking now might be the time if you do."

"Hakeem!" Darcy gushed as she studied the shimmering heart in her hand. "It's perfect," she said, lifting her face toward his. "I'll never take it off. Never."

"I'm sorry it took so long to get to you. For a while, I was scared you'd say no. And then everything fell apart. I gotta admit, though. Cooper has been pushing this for a while. Tarah too."

"Well at least they're right about this. I'm glad you listened."

"Me too." Hakeem gently took the necklace and opened its clasp. He slowly reached toward her, one end of the necklace in each hand. His palms reached up under her hair, his fingers brushing the side of her face as he worked to connect the tiny hook. Shivers went down her neck at his touch.

Darcy locked eyes with him. Black and warm, nervous but excited, intense but tender too. She could see it all and recall everything from last year to now that led to this moment.

The misunderstandings. The lost opportunities. The fear that they would never see each other again.

It all led to this second with Hakeem's fingers gently working on the back of her neck, and an electric feeling unlike anything she had ever known filling her from the inside out. She tilted her head and closed her eyes, leaning into him. A moment later, Hakeem's soft lips touched hers, brushing them gently. Darcy inhaled the scent of him, the feel of his body so close to hers, cherishing the sensation of finally being where for so long she had hoped to be.

Chapter 5

"Very nice. Much better," Aunt Charlotte said as she carefully inspected Darcy's third outfit early Saturday morning. Darcy felt awkward and self-conscious under her stern gaze. Aunt Charlotte had arrived almost an hour early with a coffee cup in one hand and her phone and jangling keys in the other. Darcy had barely finished brushing her teeth when her aunt's gold Acura pulled into their tiny driveway.

"This is a *college* program, not high school," Aunt Charlotte explained when she saw the ripped jeans and sweatshirt Darcy had planned to wear. "People are already gonna have opinions about you because of where you live and where you go to school. You show up in ripped jeans, and you'll give 'em every reason to doubt you."

"But this is what everyone's wearing," Darcy had protested.

"You're *not* everyone," Aunt Charlotte huffed. "You're a serious student who was chosen because of your potential. Dress like it."

What do clothes have to do with my potential? Darcy wanted to ask. Instead, Darcy bit her tongue and listened to Aunt Charlotte, swapping her jeans in favor of navy dress pants, a cream-colored ribbed shirt, and a navy cardigan.

"Now you look professional and respectable," her aunt said when Darcy emerged from her bedroom. "That's just what you need to make a good first impression."

"Thanks," Darcy replied, grabbing her Trinity College folder and stopping for a last look in her bedroom mirror. The necklace Hakeem had given her the other day gleamed on her neck. Seeing it almost made her forget Tarah, Cooper's party, and the nerves that made her hands slightly shaky.

Am I really going to college today? Am I ready?

Darcy left her room and paused in the hallway outside of Grandma's old bedroom as she had done a thousand times before. She wished she could speak to Grandma and tell her how anxious she felt.

"You got nothing to worry about, Angelcake. No clouds can block your sunshine," Darcy imagined Grandma saying.

Darcy savored the image as she sank into the seat of Aunt Charlotte's car and spotted her own reflection in the vanity mirror. The person she saw almost looked like someone who belonged on the campus of a fancy school, someone she could picture on the program brochure.

"Nervous?" Aunt Charlotte asked as she pulled out of the driveway.

Darcy nodded. "A little."

"I would be, too. This isn't like a class at Bluford. All the kids in this program have been chosen because they're top students like you."

Aunt Charlotte weaved skillfully through neighborhood traffic and merged onto the highway. Within seconds, the city was receding, replaced by sprawling strip malls and stretches of suburbs.

"I remember what it's like. You go from being a big fish in a small pond to . . ."

Darcy had heard the speech before. Whenever she got the chance, Aunt Charlotte would find a way to talk about her achievements. Usually she would find ways to insult Darcy's home, belittle her neighborhood, and criticize her parents too. It was as if nothing was good enough.

"It's not you," Mom explained last year after they'd had a major fight. *"It's me. Having you two girls is the one choice Aunt Charlotte approves of. But just about everything else I do is a mistake to her."*

"She's just bougie, and I got no time for that," Jamee had said. Dad had laughed so hard tears came to his eyes. The memory made Darcy smile.

"... You get to see people from all over," Aunt Charlotte droned on, "not just from down the block. College opened my eyes to ideas and places I could never have imagined. You girls need that. That's why I wanted to take you to France, remember?"

Darcy recalled last year when Aunt Charlotte mentioned taking her on a trip to Paris. It was right before Grandma's health started to deteriorate.

"I remember. I mean, it sounded exciting, but . . ." She thought of Hakeem and how they had finally gotten together. For once, she didn't feel like going anywhere.

"But what?"

"I mean there's my friends and—"

"Darcy, there's more out there for you than this neighborhood. And if you don't get out of here, you might never see it. As your Aunt, I feel it's my job to make sure you don't just stay here and miss out on the rest of the world. *That's* why I am coming with you today."

"Huh?"

"I'm not gonna lie to you. You see what happens around here. There's not a lot of opportunity. Kids make bad decisions. They get caught up in things they shouldn't. They're hanging out on the corner too late. They get shot. They get pregnant. That's not what life is supposed to be about. Not for you, not for anyone."

Darcy thought Aunt Charlotte was being unfair. Yes, there were some people who matched what she had described. She knew some of them, but they weren't all bad. And the neighborhood wasn't all bad either. Sometimes it was nice, like the evening at the park with Hakeem and the little boy. Aunt Charlotte didn't seem to understand this.

"It's not *all* like that."

"No one's saying it is, but if it's all you see, you start to think it's all there is. You might even accept that it's the best you can do. It's not! I know it might hurt to hear it, but there's gonna be a time when you need to let this place go. You're bigger than this neighborhood, Darcy, and you're going to have to leave to see how high you can fly."

"But this is my home. I like it here," Darcy protested. She tried to keep calm, but she could hear her voice rising. "I know you don't always see it, but we are happy. And even if we're not, this is our choice. This is what we've chosen."

"No, this is what your *mother* chose. But it doesn't have to be *your* choice. Twenty years ago your momma decided to rush into a relationship. Everybody tried to warn her, even your grandmother— when she wasn't on my case. But did your mother listen? No. Twenty years later and look at all the heartache and pain she's been through with your father, all the opportunities she's missed out on. She's made mistakes, Darcy. And I honestly think she's making them again." Aunt Charlotte glanced at Darcy for a split second as the car sped down the highway. "I don't want to see you stuck here because of decisions your mother made."

"Stuck? What are you saying?"

Aunt Charlotte passed a truck and moved the car out of the fast lane. Her eyes narrowed for a moment as if she thought of something unpleasant. She blinked and seemed to shrug the thought away.

"Never mind. The important thing today is you're open to new opportunities.

I'm glad you agreed to participate in this college program. And I will say this about your mother. I am glad she chose to reach out and let me take you today."

"Me too," Darcy said, hiding that it was Dad, not Mom, who suggested they call her.

Trinity College sprawled like a small city, its crimson and navy banners stretching blocks in every direction from the center of campus. A path led Darcy and Aunt Charlotte from the landscaped parking lot to a vast courtyard, called the quad, that seemed big enough to swallow all of Bluford High. The quad was dotted with crisp signs pointing to different buildings and campus locations.

Darcy couldn't help but read them all.

> Campus Commons
> Irving Student Center
> Connelly Library
> Eastwick Residence Halls
> Performing Arts Center
> Trinity Food Court

"They have a food court?" Darcy asked. *Hakeem and Coop would love that*, she thought to herself.

"They've got everything. A college like this is a whole community, Darcy. It's home for students when they're here. It's got stores, libraries, its own police department, a museum, even an ice skating rink."

"Ice skating rink? Why? I thought people were here to learn."

"They are, but Trinity has an ice hockey team," Aunt Charlotte explained. "They need somewhere to play, right? And when you're a student here, you can use it too."

Duh, Darcy thought. Of course, what her aunt said made sense, but it was all so new, so different. She had not experienced anything like it. Ever.

"Some larger universities have business schools, teacher colleges, and even full hospitals. That's where students go to become doctors. It's all out there when you're ready, and it's time you started thinking about it," Aunt Charlotte added.

Though it wasn't even ten o'clock, a coffee shop located next to the student center was packed with young adults in shorts and fleece sweatshirts, some featuring the name of the college. Others had letters that looked like the symbols in Geometry class.

"Those are Greek letters," Aunt Charlotte said. "Students wearing them belong to fraternities and sororities."

Not far away, Darcy spotted the footbridge shown in the brochure. She could see the picture had been staged to make the bridge seem bigger and more majestic than it really was. Yet, it was still fancier than anything in Darcy's neighborhood.

But there was another difference too, something that struck Darcy as she studied the students sipping coffee or chatting in small groups as they moved across campus. A striking difference from Bluford that the brochure masked.

The students, almost all of them it seemed, were white. Fair and ruddy, milky-pale to olive-hued, some freckled, others tanned, a few with blond curls, many brown-haired, and one nearby a fiery redhead, they moved about purposefully with their phones in hand and spoke in sometimes bubbly, sometimes hushed conversations.

A sea of young white people. No school Darcy ever attended was like this.

In her dark pants and cardigan, Darcy suddenly felt overdressed. She sensed that the eyes of those passing seemed to linger on her. A young man with a buzz cut, wearing cargo shorts and a polo shirt, actually stared at her as he left the coffee shop. Darcy wondered if she stood out to them as much as they stood out to her. What would they think of her?

"Relax," Aunt Charlotte said, seeming to read her thoughts. "Remember, you belong here. You earned this spot. Besides, we need to go. It's almost start time."

A short walk down a tree-lined path led them to a glass and steel building with an open lobby. A banner with a life-sized version of the brochure image greeted them.

"Bridge to Excellence," it read. *"Infinite Possibilities Await."*

Tables lined one wall and were set up next to the doorway of what looked like an oversized classroom. The tables held trays of fruit, muffins, yogurts—*Tarah hates yogurt,* Darcy thought to herself—along with bottled water and several giant silvery canisters.

"Oooh, that's just what I need," said Aunt Charlotte, pointing at the containers. "Hot coffee."

"Help yourself," said a skinny man from behind the first table. He had a boyish face and a heavy Mexican accent. Small clusters of people walked over and grabbed refreshments from the tables. Each young person was accompanied by an adult, sometimes two.

Darcy noticed this group was different from the students outside. First off, they were younger and slightly shorter. They seemed wide-eyed and more jittery too, glancing nervously at each other and at the nearby adults. Their faces were black and brown and other shades too, unlike the majority of students outside.

She remembered what Ms. Briggs said about the Bridge Program's students: *"Two high-achieving juniors from each of the city's public high schools . . ."* This meant kids from Lincoln, Zamora, West Valley, Fitzgerald, and lots of other schools.

Darcy spotted Brisana and her mother, when suddenly a voice spoke up.

"Welcome to Trinity College, everyone. Come on in," said a light-skinned woman with warm eyes and a cheerful grin. She led them into a small auditorium set up with a podium and several small round tables. A large whiteboard was positioned next to the podium. Someone had artfully written a list of topics in different colors. The terms were mostly unfamiliar, and they made Darcy's stomach sink.

Culture Shock!!!
Academic Preparation
Social Pressure
Financial Aid
Support Systems

"Good morning and welcome! I'm Jacqueline Davis, coordinator of the Bridge Program—and a graduate of Trinity College. As you can see, we've got plenty to discuss, and we'll be doing that and more for the next nine months," she said with a smile that seemed confident but also fierce. She turned from side to side as if she was trying to make eye contact with each student. "Why is there a bridge program? Because college is tough and we want you to be ready. Because we want to see you survive, thrive—and graduate!"

"That's right," Aunt Charlotte said with a nod.

Darcy looked around. The faces of the roughly thirty students in the crowd were focused on Ms. Davis's every word as she explained the purpose of the program and how it started.

"In many colleges, more than half of students drop out their first year. In the Bridge Program, we've got that rate down to just seven percent," she explained. "If your goal is to go to college, whether you choose Trinity or not, you should complete this program."

"You're listening, right?" Aunt Charlotte prodded.

Ms. Davis passed out a sheet of paper. The names of all students and their high schools were listed. Next to each name was a number from 1 to 5. Darcy had a 2 next to her name. She noticed Brisana had a 1.

Does that mean she's ranked higher than me? Darcy wondered.

"Today the adventure begins. Though we think big in the Bridge Program, we start small. And we do that by putting you in small groups. Everyone in this program is on the same team. But the people in your small group are going to become like your family. Get to know them. You'll go through the entire program together. You'll even meet during the school year. We kept students from the same school apart so you get to meet new students. And, no, the numbers don't mean anything. We just use them to keep things organized. You're all great students."

A few students chuckled as Ms. Davis pointed out the tables for each group and instructed students to gather together. She asked for parents and guardians to step outside.

"Have fun," Aunt Charlotte said with a funny smile as she left. She almost looked proud.

Darcy trudged to her group's table. A young Latina with glossy black hair, a wide, friendly smile, and piercing brown eyes stood beside it.

"Hi everybody. Please sit," she said and handed them each a sticker and asked them to write their first name on it and wear it so everyone could see. "I'm going to ask everyone to introduce themselves," she said. "Tell us your name, your school, something you're afraid of, and something you're proud of."

A few students groaned, and one boy, a white kid with auburn hair, shook his head.

"Yeah, I know. It can be a little weird, but you don't have to share anything super personal. It helps if it's something *real* though. I'll start," she explained, taking a quick breath. "I'm Marianna Lopez. I went to Zamora High, and I'm a junior here at Trinity. I'm afraid I'm going to forget all of your names, but I'm proud to tell you that I did this program when I was in high school

71

and it helped me *so much*. I wouldn't have survived college without it."

The next speaker was a girl with mahogany-colored skin whose hair was covered by a beautiful scarf of reds and golds. "I am Amina," she said softly, raising her eyes quickly before staring down at her hands. "My family emigrated from Senegal when I was twelve. I attend Lincoln High School," she continued in heavily-accented English. "I am afraid . . . that my English will not be good enough. But I am proud that it is my third language. I also speak French and Arabic."

The student next to Amina, an Asian girl with straight black hair and bangs that framed her face spoke next. "I'm Phuong," she said quickly. "My family is Vietnamese, but I was born here. I go to Ridge Valley High. What else?" She stopped, her intense black eyes glancing towards Marianna for a split second. "Oh yeah, I am proud of myself for working hard at school because . . . well, most kids at my school don't. It makes me . . . different. And different isn't always good. As for fear . . ." she paused again. "I'm afraid of feeling like I don't belong, no matter where I go." Her cheeks flushed as if she was surprised by her own words.

Darcy couldn't help but nod at the girl's honesty. It was a feeling she had until she became friends with Tarah and found herself accepted in ways she had never been before. For a second, she thought of Hakeem and wished he were at the table with her.

"I feel that way too," the boy beside Phoung said. He was short and wiry, with wavy black hair and a bad case of acne. "I'm Miguel. I'm good at math and bad at football—soccer, I mean. In El Salvador, where my family is from, it's all *futbol*. My dad wanted a soccer star and he got . . . me." Miguel grinned. "I go to Zamora. I'm proud that I'm a state math champion, but I'm afraid because in my neighborhood, that makes me a target."

"Your family's from El Salvador?" asked the round-faced girl sitting next to Darcy. Her voice was musical and warm, and she was a little on the chubby side. Her hair was pulled into a side-braid that stretched down to her waist, and she wore a leather jacket with colorful images painted on the sleeves. "Mine's from Guatemala!"

"Hello, neighbor!" Miguel laughed and shook hands with her.

"I'm Isabella," the girl continued. "I go to Martindale and to be honest, I'm not afraid of much anymore. Just failure, I guess!" She shrugged her shoulders and projected strength that reminded Darcy of Tarah. "I'm proud of this jacket," she added. "It's my favorite. I made it."

"No way!" Phuong reached out and caressed the leather. "You made that?"

Isabella nodded.

"That's sick," Miguel agreed. "You ever make things for other people? I'd pay you—"

"It *is* gorgeous, but two people in our group haven't spoken yet." Marianna smiled in Darcy's direction. "Let's give them their turn."

"My bad," Miguel said, putting his hands up to show he meant no foul. Darcy took a deep breath.

"I'm Darcy. I go to Bluford and I'm proud—well, just to be here. A lot has happened lately, and . . . I guess I'm just glad I made it."

A few students at the table nodded as Darcy thought about her answer to the next question. Nerves made her stomach feel like a bowl of worms. What came to her mind wasn't something she wanted to share, but the others had been so honest. It didn't seem right to say something stupid or fake. After an agonizing pause, she decided to be real. "And I'm afraid being here will change things . . . between me and some of my friends."

"You stole my answer," the kid next to her said after a moment's pause.

Darcy had noticed him when they first sat down together. He was the only white person in their group. He had pale freckly skin and hair that couldn't decide if it was red or brown. His blue eyes were large, and he blinked a lot as if he were struggling to absorb what he was learning. He wasn't handsome, Darcy thought, but there was something about his face that was tough to ignore, like a movie poster where the eyes seem to follow you no matter where you are standing.

"I'm Aaron. Yes, some call me A-A-Ron, and you can too, if you want." He paused as a few people in the group laughed. "I go to Fitzgerald. Bluford just beat us in football, so I guess me and Darcy got problems. We're going to meet in the parking lot and throw adverbs at each other after this, right Darcy?" he joked, blinking his big owlish eyes.

It was such an odd, quirky thing to say. Darcy shook her head and smiled. Phuong did too.

"I was gonna say I'm proud to be here and afraid to lose all my friends. You wouldn't believe how popular I am back at Fitzgerald," he deadpanned, gazing at each person at the table. "No, actually I'm not popular at all. Try not to be shocked." He rolled his eyes dramatically.

"Try being a math champion," Miguel chimed in, and the two exchanged a fist bump.

"Seriously, what I'm afraid of is that I won't be able to finish this program," Aaron admitted. "You're looking at him, folks: The kid most likely to drop out!"

He said it with lots of energy, as if it was another big joke. But Darcy saw how his face grew suddenly serious. Marianna must have seen it too, because her smile disappeared.

"Thanks for saying that, Aaron. Because it's really important. I know you've all read your packet, but this seems like the time to say something about the program's absence policy. You can miss three times— just three. During the school year or the summer, it doesn't matter. You miss three sessions and you're out, no excuses."

"But what if, I don't know, you get sick or something happens?" Miguel inter-rupted.

Marianna sighed. "The program is try-ing to prepare you for college. In college, if you miss too many classes, you won't pass. It's the same way here. You have to take it seriously. I'm not sure I agree with how they do it, but I've seen people get kicked out for absences. Don't be one of them." The seriousness in Marianna's face made her seem older.

A wave of silence gripped the table as her words sank in.

"Let's face it," she added. "None of us come from homes like the ones you passed on the way here. College is a culture shock for us. That's why this program has these groups: so you can support and encourage each other. So you can help each other overcome obstacles. It works. I've seen it. I've lived it." She paused again before continuing.

"I'm not gonna lie to you. College is hard. Not just the tests and the applications and the financial aid. But the moving away from family and joining a very different community. Those things you're afraid of—losing friends, being alone, the pressure of being the first in your family to get a college degree—it's all real."

"And this program helped you?" Amina asked.

"Oh yes! In my group, we supported each other no matter what. We used to get together any time we could. We still do." She turned to Aaron. "When one of our group got in trouble, the rest of us got together to support her. To study and share information or just to talk. Like I said, I would not have made it this far without this program. That's why I'm a discussion leader today. As a way of paying it forward, you know?"

Another blanket of silence spread over the table.

"So what you're really saying is, we're stuck with each other?" Aaron asked, grinning.

Marianna nodded. "Yes, A-A-Ron, that's exactly what I'm saying."

"Cool. Let's exchange phone numbers. Right now," he said, pulling out his phone. "Come on, come on, Group Two!" he urged until everyone including Darcy had their phone on the table. "I know if I miss three meetings, I'm out, but I'm gonna try my best not to let that happen. I promise I'll have you guys' backs, the whole way. You ready for the digits, Deuces?" he asked, blinking his big eyes.

"*Deuces*?" Darcy asked.

"Yeah. Group two, number two. *Deuces*. Get it?" Aaron explained, holding out two fingers. His eyes were playful and bright.

"That's really corny," Marianna scoffed while several others shook their heads.

"That name is horrible," Miguel chimed in, smiling. "But I think it might stick."

"You're weird, you know that, Aaron?" Isabella said, crinkling her nose and smiling. "But I like you." She turned to the group. "He's right. Let's exchange numbers and figure out our first meeting, Deuces."

When the orientation ended two hours later, Darcy had five new friends, a plan to get together in two weeks, and a storm of new questions she could not begin to answer.

Chapter 6

"Well, was it a good day?" Aunt Charlotte asked as they made their way back to her car.

"It was," Darcy admitted as she crossed the Trinity College parking lot. "I wasn't sure at first. I mean it's *really* different. But meeting the Deuces was helpful."

"The *Deuces*?"

"Oh, that's what we called ourselves. Group Two," Darcy explained.

The day had exceeded her expectations. She couldn't wait to tell Hakeem what she had learned about the challenges of college and the opportunities. She even discovered Trinity offered courses in music. She wondered if Hakeem could study there too, even though he wasn't a Deuce.

"Your group needs a better name," Aunt Charlotte said as they reached her car.

"We do," Darcy agreed with a smile. She glanced at the six new contacts on her phone. "But they were all really nice." Darcy told Aunt Charlotte their names and where they were from.

"I met some of their parents," Aunt Charlotte said. "We had a good discussion about everything you're all likely to experience your first year of college. I think it'll be helpful for your parents to know, too. I'll have a talk with them. I even took notes. Honestly it was so good, I didn't even notice that they'd run late! I can't believe it's almost three o'clock—"

Three o'clock!

Darcy stared at the time on Aunt Charlotte's dashboard and then on her phone. It was 2:37 p.m.

"Oh no!" Darcy cried. "I'm supposed to meet Tarah at three!"

Aunt Charlotte frowned, her lips tightening into a look of distaste that Darcy had seen many times before.

"I'm sure she can wait a few extra minutes—"

"You don't understand. Tarah's throwing a huge surprise party tonight, and I am supposed to help set up."

81

"Tarah?" Aunt Charlotte repeated, her face twisting as if she recalled something unpleasant. "Isn't she the loud one with the long nails? You're still hanging around with *that* girl?"

"Yes. She's one of my best friends," Darcy said defensively.

"Okay, but what's she doing with her future? Where's she gonna be in five years?" Aunt Charlotte threw questions like punches. "Is she even going to college?"

"I mean, I guess. We haven't really talked about it," Darcy lied. "We're still juniors. Why does everyone expect us to have it all figured out? There's still time—"

"Trust me. That time goes quick," Aunt Charlotte snapped. "The people you surround yourself with are very important. They influence your behavior—and your expectations for the future."

Darcy rolled her eyes and stared out the window. She wished her aunt would stop talking and drive faster, but they were caught in traffic. There was nothing Darcy could do to speed the ride home and no way for her to avoid Aunt Charlotte's words.

"Jamee's a perfect example," Aunt Charlotte continued.

My aunt is making me crazy. And I'm gonna be late for Tarah!! ☹

Darcy texted Hakeem, even though she knew he was at work and wouldn't see the message.

"Remember all the problems she had? Shoplifting and running away, and God knows what else?" Aunt Charlotte lectured. "That's because she was hanging with the wrong people. Honestly, your mother wasn't much better. Does she approve of your friendship with Tarah?"

Darcy gripped the armrest in the car and glared at the crawling traffic.

Do I look like I'm in third grade? Mom doesn't decide who my friends are! she wanted to yell. Aunt Charlotte knew nothing of the many times Tarah helped her. Tarah had even been there the day Jamee had run away. She had helped look for Jamee, something Aunt Charlotte never did.

"Mom knows Tarah is good people," Darcy said simply. "I don't have to ask her permission about who my friends are."

"Maybe you should so you don't end up making the same mistakes," Aunt Charlotte huffed.

"Seriously, Aunt Charlotte, I don't think—"

"Forget it. I can see this talk isn't going anywhere."

"Fine," Darcy mumbled as Aunt Charlotte slowly merged onto the highway. It was already past three o'clock when Darcy reluctantly decided to reach out to Tarah.

Running late. Traffic. Be there soon. 😬 Darcy texted.

Hurry. Really need u, came Tarah's response seconds later.

Darcy could almost feel Tarah's anxiety through her phone. She pictured her rushing around, sweat beading on her forehead as she made final preparations. She hoped Dez was there or that Tarah called Roylin and some of the guys from the football team to help. Still, as the minutes on Aunt Charlotte's dashboard clock kept changing, Darcy felt a pang of guilt.

"I'm not gonna lie. I need you, girl," Tarah's almost desperate words came back to her. *"I want this done right. You're the only one I trust for that."*

"I'll . . . be there, I promise," Darcy had said. She still didn't understand why Tarah was so obsessed with the party, but it didn't matter. The traffic delay was forcing her to break her promise at the worst possible time.

She wished she had brought party clothes so she wouldn't have to go home to get changed. She imagined Tarah's reaction if she walked in wearing the dress pants and top.

"What are you wearing, girl? This is a party, not church!" Tarah would say.

Darcy wondered how Tarah would respond if she told her about Trinity College. Part of her was certain Tarah would not care about any of it. The thought stung her more than she wanted to admit. She sighed at the crawling traffic. There were so many things she needed to talk with Tarah about, so much they needed to hash out. After the party, Darcy decided, when Tarah wasn't so distracted, they would sit down. Tarah could finally tell Darcy what was on her mind, and Darcy would do the same. *We'll work it out,* Darcy told herself. *We have to.*

"Oh my," Aunt Charlotte interrupted her thoughts. "There's the problem."

"What is it?"

"An accident, I think."

In the distance, Darcy spotted the flashing blue and red lights of a police car and a tow truck. Cars continued to inch along. Barely. Darcy's phone said it was 3:33. Darcy could feel Tarah stressing.

"Is there another way?" she asked, turning anxious eyes toward her aunt. "Can't you try the GPS?"

"This highway is our best option. We'll have to wait it out."

Traffic. Coming, I swear! Darcy texted at 3:35.

Tarah didn't answer. She pictured her rushing around too busy to look at her phone. But as the minutes passed and Tarah didn't respond, Darcy began to have her doubts.

At 4:06, traffic finally started to move. Darcy still hadn't heard from Tarah, even though she had texted her two more times.

Is Tarah okay, Darcy wondered, *or is she angry*?

"Can you drop me off at Tarah's?" she asked her aunt as they neared home. "I promised I'd be there almost an hour ago—"

Just then Darcy's phone buzzed with a text. Relieved, Darcy looked at it, expecting it to be Tarah, but instead it was Jamee: where are u? need you here now!!!

Going to Tarah's! Darcy's thumbs worked quickly to send the reply.

no. come home now. important

What is it?

JUST COME HOME!

It was just past 4:30 p.m. when they finally arrived. Aunt Charlotte had barely stopped when Darcy bolted from the car and rushed inside.

Mom was curled on the sofa, her face blotchy, her eyes red and swollen. Crumpled tissues were strewn around her on the floor. Dad sat next to her, hunched forward, elbows on his knees, arms crossed as if he had just been punched in the stomach. Jamee hunkered nearby on Grandma's old chair, still wearing her cheerleading uniform from the afternoon's basketball game. Her eyes were glassy and she was biting her bottom lip as if she was trying not to cry.

"What's wrong?" Darcy asked. The room was somber and quiet except for Mom's sniffles. It reminded her of the day Grandma died.

"What happened?" Aunt Charlotte spoke up from behind Darcy. She eyed the room carefully. "Did he hurt you?"

Dad glared at her, a flash of anger in his eyes. Darcy's mother shook her head.

"No," she said, her voice heavy with emotion. "It's the baby."

Darcy felt her stomach drop. In all the excitement of Trinity College and the worries about Tarah's party, she had forgotten Mom's doctor appointment.

"What is it?" Darcy blurted out, unable to stop herself. "Tell us."

Mom took a deep breath as if she needed to steel herself for what she was about to say.

"I-it's a little boy, Darcy," she began, her voice quivering. "He's a boy."

A brother, Darcy thought. *I'm going to have a little brother.*

"B-but the tests . . ." Mom continued, "they show he has a problem."

"What do you mean? What kind of problem?"

Mom clutched a tissue to her face and looked over to Darcy's father as if she didn't want to say the words.

"He's got Down Syndrome," Dad answered.

Aunt Charlotte winced.

Down Syndrome. Darcy had heard the term in biology class last year. It was a problem with an extra gene or something.

"You keep saying that, but what does it really mean?" Jamee asked, getting up from Grandma's chair and sitting on the end of the couch.

"It's a birth defect," Aunt Charlotte chimed. "It means . . ."

"It means he won't be a normal child," Dad said, his voice heavy and broken. "His brain won't grow like yours did. He won't be able to learn or understand things like we do. And there might be serious physical problems with his heart and muscles."

"But is there medicine? Can they fix it?" Jamee asked. Her eyes met Darcy's as if she was looking for support. A sign of hope.

"No," Dad continued, sighing sadly. "It's not like that, Jamee. This isn't a disease he can outgrow or recover from. It's a permanent condition. The doctor said specialists can help but only so much. At best he might be able to read a little and maybe get a simple job as an adult. But at worst, he might not be able to walk or talk or hear or see. It means he's going to need a lifetime of care."

Darcy crossed the room to be next to her mother. She rested her hand on Mom's back as tears silently gathered in her eyes. The room seemed to have darkened since they had arrived, as if someone had turned off the lights and dimmed the sun, too. Aunt Charlotte cleared her throat.

"Is there . . . another option?" she asked.

Darcy's mother nodded sadly as her father raised his swollen, bloodshot eyes.

"Yes," he said. "They—the doctors—said we might want to think about . . . not having him."

"Not having him?" Darcy repeated, her head beginning to spin. It was all too much.

A baby brother. A birth defect, and now this. "You mean . . ."

"They mean ending the pregnancy. An abortion," Aunt Charlotte said somberly. She stood like a marble statue in the center of the living room watching Darcy's mother.

"Charlotte, I can't talk about this right now," Mom said, almost begging. "I just—"

"I understand," Aunt Charlotte said, nodding. "We won't do this now. But we need to do it soon. I'm here when you're ready. And for what it's worth, I think that's what you should do—"

"Charlotte, please," Mom pleaded.

"You need to think about your girls. Think what this could mean for them. They've already had too much to deal with, and now this—"

Her mother closed her eyes.

"She said she doesn't want to talk right now!" Jamee snapped, moving protectively between Aunt Charlotte and her mother.

"Jamee," Dad protested, but it had no effect. Jamee glared at her aunt as if she wanted to shove her out the front door.

"Go home!" she shouted. "This is none of your business—"

"Jamee!" Dad warned, his voice growing louder and more direct.

"She has no right! No one asked her—"

"Jamee, shut your mouth and sit down!" Dad roared this time, his voice booming through the small house. Jamee flinched at the sound and scowled at Aunt Charlotte as she sat down.

"No, she's right, Carl," Aunt Charlotte nodded and dropped the Trinity College paperwork on the coffee table. "No one asked me. And now's not the time. I was just reminded today of the promise of your girls," she said, sounding more sincere than Darcy had ever heard her. "I want to make sure they get their chance to succeed— both of them, even if Jamee doesn't want me to," she added.

Dad glanced down at the college paperwork, and his own eyes widened. Mom looked too, and then took a deep breath.

"Oh baby," Mom said, picking up the packet and looking at Darcy. "I'm so sorry I didn't even ask. How was your college visit today?"

Darcy shrugged. It felt as though days had passed since she had visited Trinity. Somehow it didn't seem important anymore.

"It was fine," she said.

"It was more than fine," Aunt Charlotte chimed in. "Darcy got to see what's out there. She met some new friends, and she fit right in. She'll tell you about it when she's ready."

Jamee rolled her eyes until Mom flashed her a look.

"Thanks for taking her, Charlotte. You really helped us out today," Mom said, sounding a bit more like her normal self. Dad nodded and the three of them chatted briefly about the orientation while Darcy's mind churned over everything she had just learned.

Abortion. Termination.

The words possessed a grim gravity. They pulled to her mind snippets of church sermons, talk shows, articles about protests, and rumors about girls at school who'd gone to the women's clinic to end an unwanted pregnancy. It all swirled in Darcy's mind as Aunt Charlotte gave her and her mother a hug and said that she would call tomorrow. Then she left, and

Darcy sat in the quiet living room with her parents and sister, her mind still churning.

"What's gonna happen?" Jamee asked, turning to Darcy and then their parents.

"I don't know, baby. Your father and I have to think," Mom said.

"The doctors say he might suffer, Jamee. That he might not have a happy or healthy life. He might always be in pain or in and out of the hospital," Dad explained.

"But not necessarily," Mom replied. "We see plenty of happy people with Down Syndrome at the hospital. They're all different."

"But they all have special needs, Mattie," Dad said. "I don't want to bring a child to suffer or be unable to care for himself. What kind of life is that?"

Mom nodded and gently leaned into him.

"And what about bills? Or when we get old and can't care for him? What then?"

Darcy heard the sad notes in his voice and realized what her father was saying, what his choice might be. But Mom was silent. She sat with him but was somehow alone too, as if part of her was removed, weighing the decision quietly in ways only she understood.

It's not fair, Darcy thought to herself. Not to Mom or Dad. Not to the baby.

She remembered how often Grandma used to go church, how she used to pray and insist everything happened for a reason. But Darcy never found a reason for why Grandma had her stroke and became a shadow of herself.

And Darcy could see no reason for an unborn baby to be sick.

No reason her parents should have to face such a sad and lonely choice.

No reason for any of it.

Chapter 7

Don't bother coming. I don't need you.

Tarah's text flashed across Darcy's phone. She stared at it in disbelief.

The party.

Earlier, Darcy couldn't stop thinking about it. But with the news about the baby, Cooper's surprise party had been shoved from her mind.

For an hour, Darcy had listened to her parents trying to talk their way through a maze with no exits, no safe places, no easy options. No matter where Darcy went in the small house, their words filled the air, bled into the hallways, and dominated her thoughts.

"What kind of life would he have?"

"How would we afford his care?"

"What about the girls? Is it fair to them?"

The questions stopped Darcy in her tracks more than once until she fled with Jamee into her sister's messy room and closed the door. That's when Tarah's text arrived, slicing through the jumble of Darcy's thoughts.

"Oh no," Darcy groaned. "Cooper's party. I can't believe I forgot. Tarah's never gonna forgive me."

"Just tell her what happened," Jamee suggested. "You know she'll understand. Or at least she better. I mean, how can't she?"

"Honestly, I don't know that she will. Not after everything."

"Why? What's wrong?"

"I don't even feel like explaining it right now," Darcy said.

"Fine," Jamee huffed, looking hurt.

Darcy grabbed her phone and called Tarah to explain, but she didn't pick up. Darcy tried again. Jamee eyed her carefully.

"You think she's ghosting you?" she asked as the call went to voicemail.

"Maybe."

"If she's that mad, skip the party and talk to her later," Jamee advised. "She's scary when she's angry."

Darcy hung up and dialed again, but there was still no answer. She texted Tarah a quick message:

Can we talk?

Again, there was no reply, though she could see the message was delivered. Darcy knew Tarah watched her phone constantly. She was certain Tarah had seen each call and message. Part of her felt bad she had been unable to help with Cooper's party. On a normal day, Darcy would keep calling to explain to Tarah why she didn't show up. But after everything that happened, Darcy didn't want to. Instead, something new began to pulse through her fingers: a tremor of anger.

Tarah's constant dismissal.

Her rude, one-sided comments.

Her unanswered text messages and ignored calls on this, the worst possible day.

Darcy felt like throwing her phone. She knew she had broken her promise to Tarah, but it wasn't on purpose. Yet increasingly, she felt as if Tarah had done the same to her. She had been distant for weeks. She only seemed to care about one thing anymore, Cooper's party, and had no trouble ignoring anything and anyone else. She had been mean and disrespectful about the college program. And now she didn't even try to find out why Darcy had been late. It was as if she didn't care what happened in Darcy's life, that she had stopped caring weeks ago. Or was it longer?

Darcy had bottled up these feelings and told herself Tarah would return to normal after the party, but now she wasn't sure. What if she was wrong? There was only one way to find out, one way to share her side of the story. One way to know if the damage to their friendship was as bad as she feared.

Darcy gripped her phone and rose from Jamee's chair.

"Where you going?" Jamee asked.

"The party," she said. "You coming?"

It was almost seven o'clock when Darcy and Jamee made their way to Cooper's house.

> Wish me luck. Going to Coop's party 4 hours late. Hope T doesn't kill me. Wish you were here 🖤

Darcy texted Hakeem as she and Jamee neared Cooper's street.

Even from the far end of the block, Darcy spotted Tarah's decorations on the outside of the stucco rancher where Cooper lived. A string of tiny Christmas lights had been draped around the front door and the outer wall, framing the home in glimmering lights. A banner made from what looked like a charcoal bedsheet stretched across the stoop next to the door.

Happy Birthday Coop! read the large swooping silver letters, an oversized version of Tarah's handwriting.

Speakers set up in the tiny garage behind the house pumped hip-hop music into the night air. Cooper's old pickup was parked on the street, creating a space in front of the garage where a crowd of Bluford High students were gathered, some talking and laughing while others danced. Additional lights hung between the house and the garage made the party seem festive and inviting.

Darcy wondered how Tarah managed to set up all the lights and decorations when she noticed several boys from the football team, including Steve Morris and Roylin Bailey, huddled together as if they were at practice. She figured they had helped. Here and there, Darcy saw other students she knew from Bluford, and she could see they recognized her too.

Dez, Cooper's younger brother, locked eyes with Jamee as they approached the squat metal fence that separated Cooper's yard from the sidewalk.

"Great. Just the person I did *not* want to see," Jamee mumbled under her breath. "Can we make this quick?"

Darcy nodded and opened the squeaky gate as Dez darted through the crowd and went inside. She knew Tarah and Cooper, wherever they were, would soon know she had arrived. Darcy had no idea what she'd say to Tarah, but it didn't matter. She needed to see her. Now.

Inside the house, Darcy noticed glow-in-the-dark stars had been stuck to the ceiling. All of the furniture in the living room had been moved aside to make a space for dancing. Amidst piles of confetti, a small group of students, some familiar and some complete strangers, nodded their heads and raised their hands in rhythm to the beat as a rapper, a voice Darcy didn't know, spat out a rhyme.

> *Unwoke sleepwalkers all around us*
> *   dozin'*
> *Gotta shake 'em and wake 'em.*
> *We are the chosen.*
> *I'm the live wire makin' a connection*

A compass for a world that lost its direction.

While Jamee stopped to listen and watch, Darcy weaved through the crowded living room to the kitchen, where she expected to find Tarah. Instead she nearly collided with a table holding a massive, mostly eaten cake. A portion of Cooper's face actually appeared in the icing on top. On the counter across from the table were bottles of soda, a paper plate full of leftover hamburgers, another with some cold hot dogs, and a tray with a few remaining pieces of chicken. Darcy realized Tarah had prepared an enormous feast for Cooper and managed what seemed like a thousand details. Had she done it all alone?

A twinge of guilt stabbed at Darcy's chest.

Suddenly, the screen door opened, and Cooper barged into the center of the kitchen. He was wearing a paper party hat, and there was a badge pinned to his chest that read "Birthday Boy." He reached for a hamburger when his eyes met Darcy's.

"What happened to you? Where you been?" he asked quickly, looking over his shoulder, as if he expected to see Tarah.

"Long story. Happy Birthday, Coop," Darcy said, hugging him quickly. "I need to talk to Tarah."

Cooper frowned. "Nah, I don't think that's a good idea right now."

"I know she's upset—"

"*Upset?* It's more than that, Darce. You stood her up. I ain't never seen her like this, not about you anyway."

"That's what I came to explain. There's a reason—"

"Whatever it is you got to say, I don't want to hear it!" The powerful voice slashed through the music and the noise of the party. Darcy turned to face Tarah standing in the short hallway that led to the kitchen. Her lips were pressed tight over her clenched jaw, and her chin jutted forward.

"Uh oh," someone mumbled from nearby. "Aw, *snap!*"

A girl standing in the doorway where Cooper had just entered pulled out her phone as if she wanted to film them.

"Tarah, please. I'm so sorry." Darcy began. "I would have been here, but—"

"Girl, save it. You got no place here. I'm done with you."

"Tarah, I said I'm sorry. I was planning to be here, but—"

"But what? Your *college* stuff keep you late?" Tarah said the word *college* as if it disgusted her. "I don't even want to hear it."

"It wasn't that—"

"Darcy, I have never asked you for *anything*. For months I listened to every dumb little thing you needed to talk about, even when you were goin' on and on about Hakeem all summer. I tried to be excited about this college thing, even though whenever you talk about it, it's like you can't wait to leave us all behind—"

"That's not true!" Darcy yelled as Tarah moved closer. Her words, *dumb little thing*, were like stabs. Darcy was shocked Tarah had said them. The kitchen seemed to have grown smaller, as if the walls shrank inward so that Tarah and Darcy were cornered. People nearby crammed close to see what would happen next.

"Tarah—" Cooper tried to cut in but was immediately silenced.

"No, let me finish!" Tarah snapped. She took a deep breath and when she continued, her eyes were glistening, and there was hurt in her voice. "I *needed* you, and I told you that. It's the one thing I asked. And you weren't there. So if that's how it is, I'm done."

103

"Tarah, listen—"

"No, Darcy, *you* listen!" Tarah fumed. "You *promised* me. Maybe that don't mean much to you, but it means everything to me. You didn't even show up until I told you *not* to be here. I bet you completely forgot with all your *college* stuff. Like I said, you can't wait to leave us behind."

"Tarah, you got it all wrong," Darcy protested, reeling from Tarah's tirade.

"You know what? I don't even care no more." Tarah's voice sounded different, like something broke inside, as if something she once believed in was no longer true. "I been doing a lot of thinking about stuff lately. About my life and things that have happened to me . . ."

"Come on, T," Cooper said gently, moving to her side. "You don't need to do this now. It's a party, remember?"

Tarah blinked as if she was forcing back tears, but then pressed forward.

"I been realizing that some of the stuff I been doing isn't the best for me," she said, nodding to herself. "And I'm—I'm seeing this friendship maybe isn't what I thought it was, Darcy. Took me awhile, but I gotta admit it's always been one-sided. Me doing all the givin', you doin' all the taking."

"*What?*" The air suddenly felt too hot to breathe. Waves of anger and hurt boiled through Darcy, searing her insides. "Tarah, you don't even know what you're talking about."

"Oh, I know all right. I see you. The truth is, Darcy, you're kinda selfish. All you care about is *your* stuff, your future, your college plans. You ain't got time for nothin' else. When's the last time you even asked me about me—about anything I'm going through?"

"I try and you shoot me down every time, remember? All you ever talk about anymore is this *stupid* party—" Darcy winced as the words flew from her mouth. She knew they were wrong and that she didn't mean how they sounded, but it was too late. They hit the room like a bomb.

Cooper recoiled as if he had been slapped hard in the face. Tarah's jaw dropped.

"That's just wrong," someone in the crowd grunted. Someone else hissed.

"Cooper, I'm sorry," Darcy said quickly, trying to control the damage. "I didn't mean that. This has nothing to do with you or this party. I just—"

"Girl, you better leave or things are gonna get ugly in here real quick," Tarah warned.

Cooper stepped in between the girls then. "Tarah, you don't wanna do this. Please . . ."

Darcy stared at her old friend, the person she had trusted with her secrets, the one who'd been there after Grandma died and Jamee had run away. Somehow a dagger had sliced deep into their friendship, had cut it to the bone. Looking at Tarah, Darcy didn't know how it started, or where it came from or how to stop it. And after everything Tarah said and the sadness of the day, Darcy wasn't sure she wanted to.

"C'mon, Darce," Jamee said, tugging on her arm. "We should go."

Darcy eyed Tarah, her jaw locked and tight, and then looked at Cooper. He nodded yes at Jamee's words, even as he stood in Tarah's way.

"Hey, y'all, turn Savon's music back up! Everything's cool," Dez yelled into the crowd. "This is supposed to be a party."

Bass pulsed into the air, and people began to leave the crowded kitchen.

106

Darcy turned, lowered her head, and shouldered her way out into the cool black night.

Chapter 8

Hours later, Darcy stared up at the ceiling of her bedroom, rehashing what happened at Tarah's. The house had grown dark and quiet, the room strangely fuzzy, when she heard a voice.

"You're gonna have to find your path, Angelcake," a familiar voice whispered. *"Not everyone is gonna like it, but that's okay. It's your path, not theirs."*

"Grandma?" Darcy turned to see her grandmother sitting at the foot of her bed, her eyes sparkling like stars in the dark bedroom.

"It won't be easy. Sometimes it's lonely. Sometimes people will say you're making a mistake. Even your family and friends. I remember how confused I was, and I didn't have half the choices you have. So many choices."

"I don't know what to choose, Grandma." Darcy found herself whispering back in a sleepy haze.

"You will. You got time. You're still getting started. Just remember who you are and where you come from. Do that, and you'll make this world better, no matter what path you choose. And you'll make me proud."

Grandma was a silhouette at the edge of her bed, her form so light Darcy couldn't feel any pressure or weight on the mattress.

"But Tarah. She hates me now. I messed up with her."

"Oh, you two'll figure it out. We all go through rough patches. Friends got to tell each other the truth. Listen to hers, and tell her yours, and you'll be all right."

For a second, it felt like old times when Darcy was young and Grandma would sit on the edge of the bed and chat about the day and whatever was on her mind. It had been years since they had talked this way, and yet it was happening again. How?

"How are you here, Grandma?" Darcy asked. Her grandmother seemed to turn to her in the dark, the way she had done countless times when she wanted to make a point. "How . . ."

"I never left, Angelcake."

"But—"

"Now get some sleep…"

"Wait, Grandma!" Darcy sprang up from her bed, her heart pounding as she reached out to where her grandmother had been sitting. "Wait!"

But Grandma was gone, the house silent. Shadows blanketed her room. The space where Grandma had been seconds earlier was a void in the darkness. Darcy realized she must have fallen asleep, but she didn't feel as if she had been dreaming.

Had Grandma really been there?

Darcy rubbed her eyes and grabbed her phone off the mattress. The clock said it was 3:22 a.m. The words *3 new messages* glowed in the darkness. She hoped to see texts from Tarah apologizing for what she had said. Maybe there was some way they both could take back the ugly words and undo the damage they caused, though Darcy didn't know how.

"Friends got to tell each other the truth," Grandma had said. But that's what Tarah did, Darcy realized, and it had all but killed their friendship.

"The truth is Darcy, you're . . . selfish. All you care about is your stuff . . . You ain't got time for nothin' else."

Tarah's words clawed at Darcy in the dark. As much as she knew Tarah had been unfair, she also knew she had been right, or at least partly right. And in the solitude of her quiet bedroom, that truth stung like an open wound.

Darcy swiped her phone to read the texts. They were all from Hakeem.

OMG, Darce! Coop just told me what happened. Call me! he texted at 11:15 p.m.

The second text came at 11:32: Where are you? You OK? Tarah is cray and wrong.

A final message had arrived just after midnight: So tired. Looong day. Gotta go to bed. Working tomorrow until closing. I smell like popcorn. Never want to see butter sauce again. Talk later. Hope you're OK. ♥ Darcy reread the messages a few times before responding, sleepiness tugging at her in the heavy silence.

Do you think I'm selfish? she began to write but then deleted the message. Instead, she sent Hakeem a thumbs up emoji followed by 😴 before dropping her phone, the events of the day playing in her mind uneasily as she drifted back to sleep.

Tap, tap, tap.

Darcy heard the urgent knocking on her bedroom door before she had even opened her eyes.

"Darcy?" Mom called from the hallway. "You up?"

"Sort of," she groaned, wincing against the sunlight that streamed through her window. Her phone said it was almost nine o'clock. "Is something wrong?"

"No, nothing's wrong. I just decided to visit Grandma this morning, and I wanted to know if you'd like to come."

"Visit Grandma?"

"Yeah. I think it's time we went to the cemetery. It's been four months since she passed. We haven't been there as a family since a week after the funeral. I need to go, and I wondered if you want to go too."

Darcy glanced at the spot where her grandmother appeared the night before. In the daylight, her room seemed different, as if the moment with Grandma had never happened. Of course, it had been a dream, she told herself. It had to be. But the fact that Mom was choosing to visit the cemetery only hours later struck her as strange. Were the two connected?

"Yeah, I'll go," Darcy agreed.

"Me too," Jamee hollered in the distance.

The ride in the car was quiet as Dad drove first to SuperFoods and picked up a small bunch of flowers and then headed north toward Eternal Valley Memorial Park where Grandma was buried.

Jamee sat wedged against the corner of the backseat opposite Darcy, her eyes concealed by oversized silvery sunglasses. The only reason Darcy knew she was awake was that her fingers darted across her phone from the moment she sat down.

"Who are you texting?" Darcy asked finally as they neared the cemetery.

"Dez," Jamee said tilting her phone for Darcy to see. "He's on Snapchat."

"You two are talking again?"

"Not really. But after last night, I had to set the record straight. Now he knows what happened and why we were so late—and why Tarah was wrong to go off on you like that," Jamee explained. There was something new in her voice, a sound Darcy hadn't heard before. She seemed almost protective.

"I don't need you fighting battles for me," Darcy said as Dad turned the car into the entrance of the cemetery. "But thank you."

"What battles? Something happen between you and Tarah?" Mom asked, peering at her through the rearview mirror. Darcy could see her hands were resting on her swollen belly.

113

"Nothing!" Darcy said, perfectly in time with Jamee.

"Did you hear that?" Dad asked, his eyes wide open in an exaggerated expression of surprise. "Did they just agree on something? That never happens."

"Yeah, it makes me wonder what they're hiding," Mom replied as Dad parked the car.

"It's fine," Darcy insisted. "We're not hiding anything." But even as she spoke, Darcy wondered if what Jamee texted would reach Cooper, too. If so, Tarah would know it soon, Darcy figured. Maybe she was learning it right now.

"Mmm hmm," Mom mumbled. She pursed her lips and nodded as if she didn't believe Darcy but was willing to let it go. Darcy watched as Mom's eyes shifted toward the rolling fields that now surrounded them. They both took a deep breath before opening the car door.

A grassy grid of headstones, crosses, and granite plaques stretched out in front of them, wider than Bluford's football field. Darcy felt her stomach tighten as she remembered the afternoon months ago when she stood in the same spot under the hot sun with Hakeem and their friends and watched as her grandmother was lowered

114

into the ground. The memory sent a tremor through her body as she and Jamee followed their parents over the small rise that led to Grandma's grave.

Dad clutched the flowers in one hand and reached out with the other to steady Mom as they walked. Darcy noticed that her mother moved more slowly than usual, as if each step required extra effort. She had grown used to seeing her mother's weariness in recent days, but this walk was different, as if invisible weights rested on her shoulders, making each step forward difficult.

"Jeez. She almost reminds me of Grandma right now," Jamee murmured, shoving her cell phone in her jeans as they neared the gravesite. Darcy could see what Jamee meant. Their mother looked bent and fragile, as though she was much older than she really was. "I don't know how she's gonna do it."

"What do you mean?"

"Make her choice," Jamee explained under her breath so only Darcy could hear. "I mean whatever she does is just . . . wrong, you know? It's not fair."

Darcy nodded. She had felt the same way whenever she thought of her mother. To have the baby could lead him to a world of suffering, but to end the pregnancy would never give him a chance. But what chance would that be? Darcy didn't know. No one did. It was an awful choice that no one should have to make. A deeply personal decision that, Darcy realized, rested mainly on Mom. It reminded Darcy of Grandma's words the night before.

It's not gonna be easy.

Sometimes it's lonely.

Sometimes people will say you're making a mistake.

"Maybe that's why we're here," Darcy blurted after a few seconds.

"Huh?" Jamee asked.

"Maybe Mom needs to talk to Grandma. You know? Like we used to do?"

"I still do that," Jamee confessed. "I know it sounds silly."

"No it doesn't. I do it too," Darcy said as they approached the tree near Grandma's grave.

"You do? I thought I was the only one," Jamee whispered, sounding relieved.

"I did last night," Darcy admitted.

"For real?"

Darcy nodded. It felt strangely comforting to speak of Grandma as if she were still alive, still involved with them somehow.

"I never left, Angelcake." The words echoed in Darcy's mind.

Up ahead, her parents had stopped. They stood in the second row of stones in this quiet corner of the graveyard, a spot where the grass hadn't yet fully grown, the wound in the earth still visible.

But you did, Grandma. You did leave us. Darcy thought, looking down at the granite plaque and the etched words that were more real than anything.

Annie Luella Duncan

Mom sat down in front of the grave and tenderly touched the stone. Dad rubbed her back and placed the small bundle of flowers on the ground. After a moment, Darcy sat beside her, and Jamee followed. Overhead a gentle breeze whispered, but for a while no one spoke.

"I felt like I had to include her," Mom said, breaking the silence, her voice quivering slightly. "She would want to know what's happening, and she would want to help. You all know that's how she was."

Darcy nodded along with everyone else. Mom's eyes welled, but no tears fell as she continued.

"I'm a nurse because of her. She taught me to work hard and to help people, and

I do it every day because of her, and most days I love it. She supported me when things got rough, moving in with us when we needed help," Mom said, her voice growing stronger as she talked, as if she was finding her footing with each word.

"What's happening isn't right. It feels like the toughest decision I've ever had to make. I can't speak for no one else, and I wouldn't tell anyone what to do in this situation." Mom paused and then continued, "But for me . . . I'm a nurse. I know how to care for people, and I know good doctors. And from the start, I was scared but I *wanted* this child. Carl, I know you did too. I know how much love you have for him."

Darcy watched her father wipe his eyes, though they remained locked on Mom as if he was hanging on her every word.

"Maybe it doesn't make sense. I don't want to burden you girls or make your lives more difficult in any way. And I certainly don't have all the answers, but I have one. I want this baby, Carl. I want to have him."

Dad leaned forward as if he suddenly lost strength. He nodded, and his forehead came to rest against Mom's shoulder, as if she were holding him up. The two embraced, and as Darcy watched, she knew in her heart that she agreed with her mother's choice. She reached forward to her parents, and their arms, heavy and warm, enveloped her.

Darcy felt Jamee join them, a little late and maybe less certain, but she was there. And Darcy knew—she could feel it in her bones—that Grandma was there too.

Chapter 9

Monday morning began with the pattering of rain against Darcy's bedroom window. Bleary-eyed after a long talk the night before with Hakeem about the baby and the party, she glanced at her phone instinctively, as she had done countless times since her fight with Tarah.

"I'm sure she's gonna apologize to you. I mean how can't she?" Hakeem had said.

But there were no messages. Neither she nor Cooper had reached out since the party, and with each hour that passed, Darcy felt a wave of tension and dread building like a storm.

Is Tarah still angry?

Is she gonna make a scene at school?

Are we even friends anymore?

The questions replayed in an endless loop in Darcy's mind while she was trying to finish her chemistry lab report the night before. Yet, mixed with her worries, Darcy felt flashes of her own growing anger, too. Tarah had been mean and unfair, and her silence had added an extra layer of insult, salt in the wound.

"*Yeah, I meant what I said,*" it seemed to say. "*So whatchu gonna do about it?*"

Darcy gazed out her window, which was fogged and streaked with drizzle. She didn't know.

"You still didn't hear from Tarah?" Jamee asked at breakfast as they prepared to leave for the ten-minute walk to Bluford.

"Nope," Darcy grumbled, dreading the day ahead, especially lunchtime at their table.

"Seriously, that's messed up," Jamee blurted when they left the house. "She owes you an apology. Big time." Her words almost made it worse.

"I know."

"Tarah knows why we were so late Saturday. Dez told her straight up. He said she and Coop even had an argument about it," Jamee added as they crossed a street, "especially after someone posted a video of your fight."

"What?" Darcy exclaimed, stopping in the middle of the sidewalk. Her shoes scraped against the wet pavement with an awkward screech.

"Yep, Dez told me last night. We're kinda talking again. Anyway, Cooper took your side. Let's just say Tarah was *not* happy with him."

"Why didn't you tell me?!" Darcy fumed.

"It was late, your door was closed, and you were on the phone. I thought maybe you were talking to her."

Darcy groaned as a city bus lumbered past them. The news was getting worse, not better. "Why would someone post something like that?"

"People are stupid, that's why," Jamee sighed, hoisting her backpack higher on her shoulder. "It's like what Vanessa did to me and Angel. Remember?"

Darcy winced, recalling how the girl had spread a rumor on social media that Jamee was gay. "But Tarah wouldn't do that. That's not her."

"You sure? She's always got her eyes on her phone."

"Yes, I'm sure! I know her," Darcy insisted but then she stopped herself as she remembered the events of the last few days. "Or at least I thought I did."

She pictured Tarah stewing in anger as she watched their argument on her phone. "I don't even know what to say to her right now."

Clusters of students, hooded and sleepy-eyed in the morning drizzle, shambled passed them. The first period warning bell wailed out over the school grounds. Classes would begin in minutes. Both girls turned and picked up their pace.

"Listen, I love Tarah, and I agree with her on almost everything. But this . . . you didn't do anything wrong, Darcy. Trust me, I would tell you if you did." Jamee's eyes were locked on hers.

"I know you would. You always do."

"Hey, you do it to me too, Darce. You're worse than Mom sometimes," Jamee continued. "But after everything, I did like you said and spoke to Grandma. We got our own things to worry about. Tarah should cut you some slack. If she doesn't, maybe she's not the friend you thought she was."

"Thanks," Darcy muttered. Part of her wanted to argue Jamee's point and defend her friendship with Tarah, but another part, bogged in anger and hurt, refused. She wished she could just turn around and go home and not have to face Tarah at all.

Instead, Darcy forced herself into the crowd and followed Jamee through the metal detectors inside Bluford's front doors. Principal Spencer, always at the entrance in the morning, eyed her curiously as she passed.

Did someone share video of the fight with her? Darcy wondered.

Taking a deep breath, Darcy left Jamee and headed toward the junior class corridor. She knew Tarah and Cooper would be at his messy locker at the end of the hallway, their usual spot before class. Her heart raced and her palms grew clammy as she weaved through hall traffic toward them.

But Cooper and Tarah weren't there. The hallway seemed strangely empty without them.

Were they late?

Darcy imagined Cooper taking too long to get ready and Tarah complaining about it. She had seen it a thousand times but not usually in the morning. Just then, Hakeem darted toward her locker, his clothes slightly wet, his eyes narrowed with concern.

"You see Coop?" he asked before she had even said hello.

"No. Why?"

"He and Tarah had a big fight," Hakeem explained, wiping the moisture from his face. "He wouldn't talk about it with me, and he left early. Real early. I never seen him this upset."

"Did you try texting him?"

Hakeem nodded. "He's not answering."

"Me and Tarah are the same way. I haven't heard a word from her since Saturday!"

"I heard him leave way before school this morning, but he never came back. Dez and I had to ride bikes to school. That's why I'm late. It's not like him to be this way."

RING!

The final warning bell blared overhead. Darcy knew they had just a moment to get to class. She grabbed the chemistry book from her locker and pulled out her phone.

"I gotta run, or I'll be late," Hakeem said, giving Darcy a quick kiss that made her heart skip.

"Meet me at lunch," she called out as he rushed off. She raced up the stairs to chemistry class, texting Tarah as she went.

Where are you? she wrote, reaching Ms. Allen's classroom as the first period bell rang.

"Cutting it close, Ms. Wills," the teacher said with a tight-lipped smile from her desk. She then got up and handed Darcy a folded sheet of paper. Darcy grabbed it and retreated to her seat before opening it. She recognized the quiz she had completed last week, only now it was marked in Ms. Allen's slanted handwriting.

A score was circled in pen in the top right corner: 96. Beneath it, a handwritten comment had been scribbled in angular blue ink:

> *Good job! You know your organic chemicals, Darcy. Consider a career in medicine!*

*　*　*

The noise and chatter of the busy cafeteria seemed louder than usual as Darcy made her way to lunch. Tarah still hadn't answered her first text—or the second and third ones Darcy had sent during Algebra 2.

You OK? The words in her final message hung empty and incomplete in her phone.

Maybe this is it, Darcy thought. The end. After a year, Tarah may have finally decided to cut her friendship off, once and for all. Maybe Tarah had nothing more to say to her.

Darcy knew it was possible.

Fine, she grumbled to herself. If Tarah had reached that point, she would accept it. But there was something she needed to say first.

"*Tell her your truth.*" Grandma's words echoed in her mind. Darcy knew it wouldn't be easy, but she had no choice: She had to be honest and tell Tarah how much her actions had hurt.

"There you are!" cooed a familiar sing-songy voice as she waited in line. Darcy turned to see Brisana circling toward her, a knowing grin on her face. "I've been looking for you. Wasn't Saturday amazing?"

"What do you mean?" Darcy asked as Brisana joined her.

"Trinity College! *Hello!*"

"Oh, yeah, that . . ." Darcy replied. The Bridge Program felt as if it had taken place weeks ago.

"*That*?!" Brisana scoffed as if Darcy said something silly. "You mean the competitive program that could get us a full ride to college? No big deal, right?" Brisana joked.

"Sorry, Bris. It was a long weekend, and I've got a lot on my mind and—"

"Oh, I heard all about your weekend!" Brisana cut in, her face suddenly lit up as if she had just listened to gossip that greatly interested her. "I can't believe her." Brisana gave a smug nod to Tarah's empty seat.

"What did you hear?"

"Not just what I heard, but what I *saw*. The clip of you and Tarah almost getting in a fistfight at Cooper's party." Brisana's eyes sparkled as if the incident made her happy.

"It wasn't that bad," Darcy huffed.

"It looked pretty bad to me. I was like 'Wow' 'cause I thought she was actually gonna hit you. I wouldn't put it past her." Brisana shook her head as if she were about to gloat. "I know she's your friend and all, but—"

"Don't, Brisana," Darcy warned. "I know what you're gonna say, and I can't hear it right now."

"Okay, okay. Relax, girl. I get it," Brisana said, pausing as if she were trying to solve a puzzle. She reminded Darcy of a chess player searching for the best move.

"I can't believe you went from visiting a college to dealing with ghetto nonsense all on the same day." She watched Darcy's reaction carefully. "I hope Ms. Briggs doesn't see that video, or she's gonna wave her crazy bracelets at you and be like '*Don't throw this away*.'" Brisana imitated the guidance counselor's voice and rapidly moving hands.

Darcy clenched her teeth. She didn't want Brisana to know that her words cut like a knife. Darcy knew a fight on social media wasn't going to help her get into college—or anywhere, except trouble.

"Are you done?" Darcy finally grumbled.

"Well it's not all bad news. I heard you have an admirer in the Bridge Program," Brisana teased.

"What?"

Brisana went into a long story about her day at Trinity College while Darcy grabbed a tray of greasy French fries and spongy chicken nuggets. They were just returning to the table when Brisana explained that Chelsea, a girl in her group, goes to Fitzgerald High School and is classmates with Aaron.

"So?" Darcy asked her.

"So . . . he likes you. That's what Chelsea said."

"You mean A-A-Ron?" Darcy asked in disbelief. "The nerdy white boy with all them corny jokes? Him? Oh my God!"

"I know, right? Don't worry. I told her he wasn't your type," Brisana said, as if she were proud of herself.

"Why did you do that?"

"What, am I wrong?" Brisana asked as if Darcy had spoken a strange foreign language. "I thought I was doing you a favor."

"No, you weren't wrong, but that's not the point. I don't need you speaking for me. Especially there. Like you said, let's not carry over stupid high school drama into college. Okay?"

"Whatever. He's weird. Besides, Chelsea says his sister's disabled or retarded or something . . ."

Retarded or something.

The comment snagged in Darcy's mind like a jagged rusty nail, but Brisana didn't seem to notice. She kept talking as Darcy's pulse began throbbing in her neck.

". . . said he almost skipped the program because he takes care of his sister on weekends so his mom can work. Talk about drama. I'd stay far away from that," Brisana continued.

Darcy's insides recoiled.

Retarded or something.

Would Brisana use those words to describe her brother one day? Darcy wondered. She wouldn't be alone. Others would probably join in at some point once the baby is born.

"I'm just glad we both got chosen," Brisana continued. "We finally get to see what's out there and meet other people who are actually gonna be somebody. People like us. Just like old times, right?"

Darcy stopped listening. A world of challenges loomed ahead. Darcy saw glimpses of it in the new faces at Trinity College, but there was so much more. The baby was going to change her family. She was just beginning to feel it. If what Brisana heard was true, Aaron was living it already or something like it. Maybe he could teach her something, help her prepare? Darcy would find out one day, but she had to do something first. Her eyes twitching, her hands trembling, she turned and glared at Brisana.

"There is no *us*, Brisana," she said calmly.

"What?"

"I need you to leave. Now."

"What's wrong with you all the sudden? What'd I do?"

"You're just being . . . you, and I can't deal with it right now. Goodbye."

Brisana looked as if she had been punched. Students at nearby tables watched, but Darcy didn't care. She held up a hand and waved it slowly while mouthing a single word that anyone in the cafeteria could see.

"Goodbye."

Just then, Hakeem entered the far side of the cafeteria with the same tense look he had earlier. He watched Brisana storm off as he sat down.

"What was that about?"

"Never mind. Have you heard from them yet?" she asked, gesturing to where Cooper and Tarah usually sat.

"They cut school today."

"Are you serious?"

In all the time she had known Tarah, Darcy had never seen her miss school. Even when she was sick, Tarah came to class. It was something she was proud of. For her to be absent meant something was wrong. Seriously wrong.

Despite all the frustration and anger, Darcy felt a gnawing feeling, one she could not silence or ignore.

Tarah needed her.

Now.

Chapter 10

"Are you sure you want to do this?" Hakeem asked. They huddled together at Darcy's locker at the end of the day. His eyes were urgent and sincere. "You know what happened the last time you saw Tarah. What makes you think it's gonna be any different now?"

"I *have* to see her," Darcy insisted. She had made her choice in the cafeteria and thought about it all afternoon. "If she's gonna cut me off, what do I have to lose? And if something's really wrong with her, maybe I can help. Either way, we need to settle this."

The crash and boom of slamming lockers thundered like war drums in the hallway.

"Maybe it's better if you give her space. Leave her alone until she calms down. I don't want a repeat of Saturday night."

"Neither do I," Darcy admitted, leaning her head into Hakeem's chest. "I don't want to fight Tarah, but I don't want to lose her either. What if something's really wrong?"

"*Wrong?* Like what?"

Darcy pulled away and grabbed her book bag.

"I don't know. She hasn't been acting herself. You've seen it too. I know you have." Darcy shut her locker and joined the crowd heading toward the exit.

"Yeah, but that's just how Tarah is sometimes. I asked Coop, but he told me it was nothing." Just then Hakeem's phone chimed.

"Speaking of Coop, he's finally replying. It's about time," Hakeem stared at his phone for an instant and stopped in the middle of the hallway. "Uh oh. This isn't good."

"What?"

"Coop's home now. He says he and Tarah broke up today."

Broke up.

The words shook Darcy like a small earthquake. She leaned in and stared at Hakeem's phone, rereading Cooper's message several times to make sure it was real. Another arrived as she watched.

I'm not good bro, it read. Not good at all.

The hallway seemed to sag beneath Darcy's feet. Voices of nearby students faded, and time seemed to pause as Darcy digested the somber news.

No couple seemed more perfect or more meant for each other. Tarah and Cooper had been together so long, Darcy couldn't imagine them any other way. They were supposed to be forever. How could this happen?

Darcy shoved aside the anger and resentment that had gathered since Saturday. She knew where she had to be.

"That's it," Darcy barked. "I'm going to Tarah's house right now. And you go talk to Coop. He needs you." Darcy bolted from Bluford High School, not looking back.

Tarah lived a short bus ride from school in a mint green ranch house she shared with her mother and, at times, her cousin and niece. From the bus, Darcy noticed Tarah's house stood out on the street. A black metal fence surrounded the tiny front yard, separating the property from the sidewalk. The windows and doors were also clad in black metal bars, making the house look protected, but also caged.

Though it was only 3:15 p.m. when Darcy stepped off the bus, the dreary sky made it feel much later. The drizzle from earlier had ended, but clouds had lowered and thickened into a heavy overcast that blanketed the sky.

Darcy was surprised to see Tarah's mother's car parked in the small drive-way. Darcy knew she worked full-time as a prison guard, a job that kept her out of the house most days until well past five o'clock.

Why is she home now? Darcy wondered.

Taking a deep breath, Darcy opened the gate, stepped nervously to the front door, and pressed the doorbell. She heard the electronic chimes echo through the house, followed seconds later by the stomp of approaching steps. The front door creaked open to a solid, barrel-shaped woman nearly as tall as Darcy's father. Her eyes, wary and bothered at first, softened as soon as they spotted Darcy.

"Hi, Ms. Carson," Darcy said, trying to hide her concern. "I was wondering if I could see Tarah. Is she home?"

Tarah's mother eyed her intently. Darcy felt as if Ms. Carson was studying her face, searching for clues about her intentions.

"You know, she wasn't feeling well ear-lier today, Darcy," she said finally. "But I think it would do her some good to see you. C'mon in. She's in her room."

"Tarah," she called out. "You have a visitor."

"I told you I don't wanna see nobody," Tarah yelled in the distance.

"Go on back," Ms. Carson urged. "It's okay. You'll be good for her."

"Tarah?" Darcy called, knocking gently on the half-closed bedroom door before walking in. She found Tarah hunched on her bed. An old maroon photobook sat closed at the foot of her mattress. Tarah held a tissue box on her lap and her phone at her side. Her eyes widened when they met Darcy's.

"Oh no. Tell me you didn't just walk up in here," Tarah sniffled. She shook her head almost in disbelief, but Darcy noticed something else there too. Gratitude and a weak smile.

"I didn't walk. I took the bus," Darcy tried to joke.

"Girl, you are crazy."

"Answer my texts next time, and I won't have to barge in on you."

Darcy sat down on the edge of the bed. She noticed Tarah's eyes were puffy and bloodshot. Even now, tears were welled in them. Darcy ached seeing her so sad, but she didn't know why, not exactly. "Are you okay?"

Tarah shrugged and took a deep breath. Darcy had never seen her look so vulnerable, so fragile.

"I've had better days. Mom and I just got home from . . . a meeting. Used to go with Coop, but I guess I won't be doing that no more."

"A meeting?" Darcy ignored the mention of Cooper for a second, letting Tarah choose what she wanted to say, listening to her.

Tarah stared at Darcy for a long time, as if she were searching for an answer to some impossible question, an escape she could not find. Then she turned away.

"I'm kinda surprised you're even here," Tarah said finally, changing the subject. "After all the stuff I said Saturday night."

"Tarah, we don't need go into that now—" Darcy began, but Tarah held up her hand.

"No, we do," she interrupted. "Before you say anything, Darcy, I gotta say I'm sorry. I shoulda known you had good reason for being a no-show. I felt so bad when I heard about your baby brother. I'm sorry for coming down on you the way I did, and I'm sorry some triflin' fool put us on YouTube."

"I'm sorry, too, Tarah."

"You don't got nothing to be sorry for. It wasn't your fault. If my mom was in that situation . . ." she sighed heavily, wagging her head from side to side. "What I did ain't right."

"But I've been wrong too. I didn't want to admit it, but inside I knew it. I am so sorry, Tarah," Darcy insisted.

Tarah looked up at her, confusion pushing aside the sadness for a second. "What do you mean, Darcy?"

"What you said before. About me being selfish—"

"I said a bunch of mean things I shouldn't have said."

"But I knew there was something wrong, Tarah," Darcy confessed. "You've been acting so different. Angry one minute, distracted the next. You'd say odd things sometimes, but then we'd never talk about it. You know?"

Tarah nodded and wiped her eyes.

"I kept telling myself if it was a really big deal, you'd talk to me. But I shoulda asked more. I shoulda acted like it mattered because it *does*," Darcy insisted. "And then when things got crazy at home and with Hakeem and school, I let it go. That's no excuse, and for that I'm sorry, Tar. I know sometimes it doesn't seem like it, but I care about you *so much*, girl. And I'm here for you. I might not be as good at giving advice as you are, but I can listen."

Tarah covered her face with her hands. Quiet sobs shook her body. Darcy moved close and embraced her.

"What is it, Tarah?" Darcy asked urgently. "What's wrong?"

Tarah hunched in her bed, her arms around her knees, her head bowed as if she were under the weight of some immense unspoken pain. Unsure how to comfort her, Darcy sat close, gently rubbing her back until gradually the hurt seemed to ease, the sobs calmed. Finally, Tarah lifted her head, her eyes tired and bloodshot.

"My meeting today," Tarah said at last, "was with a counselor. She's been helping me for a few months now. Coop's been taking me."

"*A counselor?*"

"I needed help. The panic attacks and lost sleep were killing me. It might not seem like it, but I'm better than I was. I'm getting through it. One day, when I'm ready, maybe I'll tell you about it. For now, all I'm gonna say is remember what almost happened to you with Brian Mason? Remember what he almost did to you?" Tarah's eyes glimmered with black fire.

Darcy nodded recalling the afternoon he groped and assaulted her last year.

"It's like that. But worse, Darcy," Tarah said, shivering slightly at the memory. Darcy instantly understood the secret Tarah was hiding. She had been raped. She was a survivor.

"Tarah, I am sorry—"

"Don't," Tarah said, holding her hand out as if to say stop. "Like I said, I am getting through it. And I'm learning a lot about myself and my relationships. I'm messed up, Darcy. I been hiding the truth for so long. Been so busy pretending to be happy that I never even got to know myself. To fix it, I need to do some work on my own. I need to step back from . . . well, just about everything . . . and everyone."

"Everyone?" Darcy repeated.

Tarah nodded slowly. "I can't have a serious boyfriend right now, even one as good as Coop. My counselor agrees. That's why I broke up with him last night. Been working up to it for a while actually," she added quietly. "It was the hardest thing I ever done. He's been so good to me, Darcy.

Too good. He deserves better, and I can't give it to him right now."

"Is that why the party had to be so perfect? Because you knew you were breaking up?" Darcy asked. Tarah's actions over the past months began to make sense. Darcy felt a sting of guilt for not knowing her friend's agony, for missing the signs for so long.

Tarah nodded slowly. "I hope one day we can get back together. But for now," she said, fixing her sad eyes on Darcy, "I need to step back from him and just about everyone."

Darcy stared back at her friend, letting her words sink in. The truth of what Tarah was suggesting began to take form and make sense. Tarah was breaking up with Cooper—but also everyone else, including her.

"Are you sure, Tarah? I mean, we're your friends. Why would you cut yourself off from the people who love you?"

Tarah stared straight ahead, not looking at Darcy.

"I need time and space, Darcy. To figure things out. Concentrate on getting myself straight and healthy. And it's hard to do that when your best friend has so much going on. I'm not mad at you, but you're going places, Darcy. You're gonna go off and be a doctor or something, but me . . . I'm just *here*. I don't know what I want to be or how to get there. Pretty soon, you're gonna move on and I'ma just be here. Stuck."

"We'll get you unstuck then, Tarah. That's what friends are for. To help each other . . . support each other. If it's school stuff, I can help. And if it's something else—"

"You sound like Coop, and I love you for it. But this is something *I* gotta do. I need to deal with myself for a while," Tarah grabbed another tissue and wiped her eyes with it. "You're my friend, Darcy. I know you are . . ." Tarah whispered. "But can you be my friend enough to leave me alone for awhile?"

Darcy's eyes burned. She felt as if her insides were being pulled apart. Tarah was asking the impossible. How could she reject what her best friend was asking? And yet how could she let her walk out of her life? It was as if a death were occurring. A death of their friendship. Their bond. Their sisterhood.

"Are you sure this is what you want?" Darcy asked. After failing her for months, Darcy felt she had no choice but to honor

Tarah's request, though every cell in Darcy's body said not to.

Tears slid down Tarah's face as she nodded.

"Yeah. I—I think it's for the best."

Tarah pushed the tissue box aside, stood up, and headed toward the hallway. "I'm glad you came over. I really am, but I think you'd better go. Ain't no point in dragging this out. It's hard enough as it is."

Darcy wanted to protest, but Tarah walked out. Darcy's legs nearly buckled as she followed her to the front door, where Tarah finally turned to face her. They stood for a second under the small awning in silence.

After so much time and so much history, Darcy never imagined their friendship ending like this. It felt wrong, a violation of something sacred and true. But Tarah had made her decision and now, Darcy knew, it was time for her to make hers.

She wrapped her arms around her friend and squeezed her tight.

"You're right. Changes are coming and we've all got our choices to make," Darcy said. "But I'm making one right now: I'm not giving up on this friendship. I'm going to keep checking on you and I'm going to be here when you're ready to talk and when you get yourself unstuck. You're not getting rid of me that easy, Tarah. You hear me?"

Tarah nodded, returning the hug. Darcy could feel the emotion in her embrace, but also her strength too. "Thanks, girl," Tarah whispered before gently pulling away.

It was drizzling again when Darcy boarded the bus home. As the streets passed, slick and gloomy in the gentle rain, Darcy's mind churned with what life had hurled at her.

Her closest friend had shut the door on their relationship. Her parents were having a baby that would change their household forever. Her relationship with Hakeem was finally blossoming. And Trinity College loomed with a world of new challenges.

Darcy couldn't see the future, couldn't tell what would happen with any of it. All she could control was the choices she made. And as she got off the bus in the slate-gray night, she knew what she had chosen, what she would always choose.

No matter what her aunt said, she couldn't leave her family or her friends. They were her past *and* future, and she would fight for them, no matter what.

But how? Darcy glimpsed an answer. It had been planted many years ago, fueled by what she had learned from Mom about working hard and helping people. It had been nurtured when she cared for Grandma after her stroke. It had been fed by success at school and her college visit. Ms. Allen's suggestion and Tarah's words earlier kindled it, too.

"*I know good doctors,*" Mom had remarked.

"*Consider a career in medicine,*" Ms. Allen had suggested.

"*You're gonna go off and be a doctor,*" Tarah had predicted.

Their voices called to Darcy and stirred something deep in her. There was so much pain in the world. Everywhere. So many wounds. Tarah had just showed her that again, igniting a spark that burned the entire bus ride and chased away the evening gloom as she walked home.

One day, Darcy would tell Tarah of this night, of the moment on the street when she first saw the path that wedded her school success with a passion to ease the pain in the world. A way to help her baby brother and her family, and honor them too. An answer to the uncertainty of the future that felt right and true and good.

Infinite possibilities await, the brochure had said.

Darcy had chosen one of them.

Dr. Wills, she thought, opening the door to her awaiting family. *I could get used to that.*

Want to know the full story about Darcy, Tarah, Hakeem, and Cooper? Read these Bluford Series books!

Jamee and Darcy are sisters, but they're not alike.

Check out these books about Jamee and her friends to see another, edgier side of Bluford High.

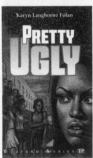

**Think boys have it easy at Bluford High?
Guess again.**

See their struggles in these gripping titles.

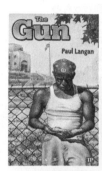

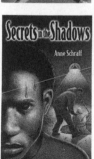

Ever imagine what it's like transfer to Bluford High, with the weight of the world on your shoulders?

Martin Luna will tell you—in his own words.

The 🆃🅿 Bluford Series

Stories to Experience

. . . and more titles coming soon!

TP TOWNSEND PRESS

Learn more about the Bluford Series
www.townsendpress.com

Listen to Bluford Series audiobooks
www.bluford.org

Follow the Bluford Series on social media

www.facebook.com/Bluford.Series/

www.twitter.com/Bluford_Series

www.instagram.com/theblufordseries/